# Enid Blyton

# The Wishing Spells

## ...and other stories

D0231329

B Bounty
Books

Published in 2014 by Bounty Books,
a division of Octopus Publishing Group Ltd,
Carmelite House
50 Victoria Embankment
London EC4Y 0DZ
www.octopusbooks.co.uk

An Hachette UK Company
www.hachette.co.uk

Enid Blyton ® Text copyright © 2014 Hodder & Stoughton Ltd
Illustrations copyright © 2014 Octopus Publishing Group Ltd.
Layout copyright © 2014 Octopus Publishing Group Ltd.

Illustrated by Lesley Smith.

ISBN: 978-0-75372-659-4

A CIP catalogue record for this book is available from the
British Library.

Printed and bound by CPI Group (UK) Ltd, Croydon, CR0 4YY

3 5 7 9 10 8 6 4

# CONTENTS

# The Wishing Spells

"Are you going to take those boots and shoes out this morning?" Ma called to little Shuffle. "Well, then, will you deliver these three wishing spells to Dame Dandy for me?"

"Right, Ma," said Shuffle. He put the mended boots and shoes into a basket and set off, whistling. The wishing spells were in a little yellow packet on the top of the boots. Shuffle kept looking down at it to make sure it was still there.

"Can't lose wishing spells," thought little Shuffle. "Very dangerous if they got into the hands of the wrong people."

Now, as he went through the wood, along came Grabbit the gnome, and with him was his sister, Mrs Well-I-Never. They both stopped at once.

"Well, I never! There's little Shuffle large as life and twice as natural," said Mrs Well-I-Never.

"Being a good boy and taking back all his mended boots and shoes," said Grabbit. "And how are all your mother's cats, Shuffle?"

Shuffle didn't like this. He began to edge away. They came closer, and Mrs Well-I-Never's sharp eyes caught sight of the little yellow packet on top of the basket.

"Well, I never! If that isn't one of Ma Shuffle's packets of spells. Let me see, Shuffle." And before little Shuffle could stop her she had snatched the yellow packet and opened it. Out came the three tiny wishing spells.

Mrs Well-I-Never knew what they were at once. "Grabbit," she said, giving them to her brother, "look here, wishing spells! We've never had any in our lives."

"Give them back," said Shuffle, feeling very uncomfortable indeed. "They won't do you any good. Ma says however much people like you are given good things like

6

wishing spells, you'll only get bad out of them. So you give them back before anything horrid happens to you."

"Are you being rude to us, Shuffle?" said Grabbit. "Sister, he's being rude. Shall we wish him away to the Land of Dustbins?"

Shuffle was scared. "Er – is it worthwhile wasting a wish on me, do you think?" he said.

"On the whole, no," said Grabbit. "Come on now, Sister, what are we going to wish for? A grand castle set up on that hill over there? My, that would make our friends stare!"

"A grand castle!" snorted Mrs Well-I-Never. "Just like a man, Grabbit. Who's going to do the work in a great, cold, draughty castle? I'm not going to live there and scrub your floors and cook your dinners, and—"

Mrs Well-I-Never could quite well go on like this for hours. Grabbit yelled at her.

"All right, all right. We won't have a castle. You think of something."

"I wouldn't mind a few new hats," said Mrs Well-I-Never. "I saw one yesterday with—" Grabbit gave such a loud snort that all the rabbits who were watching darted back to their holes.

"Hats! *Hats*! Just like a woman. What do you want a hat for with a head like yours, and a face like—"

"Mr Tappit's goat," said little Shuffle, before he could stop himself.

"*Oh*!" said Mrs Well-I-Never, in a rage. "Well-I-never! Well-I-never-did-in-all-my-life! Grabbit, we must use a wish on

8

Shuffle. We must, we must. What shall we wish? Shall we wish him into an earwig and tread on him? Shall we wish him into a worm and call that fat thrush down? Shall we wish him into a nail in our shoes and walk on him all day long? Shall we—?"

"Hold your tongue," said Grabbit, impatiently. "You're full of crazy nonsense. Always have been. I do wish, for once in your life, that you'd be sensible."

Shuffle gave a squeal of laughter. All the watching rabbits pricked up their ears.

"Now what's so funny?" demanded Grabbit.

"You've wished a wish," said Shuffle, grinning. "You wished she'd be sensible for once."

Mrs Well-I-Never gave a scream. "Yes, you did! You did! Look at the wishing spells in your hand. One's gone!"

Grabbit looked. Yes, there were only two wishing spells left now. Mrs Well-I-Never grabbed at them and got them.

"There now, you can't waste any more. I've got them both. You be careful, Grabbit. I've got two wishes here, you just be careful."

Grabbit lost his temper. He ran at his sister and she screamed and ran between the trees. "Don't shake me! Don't! Oh, Grabbit, I wish you'd go away."

Shuffle gave another squeal of laughter. Mrs Well-I-Never looked at him. "Now what's the matter with you?"

"He's gone. You wished him away," said Shuffle. "I say, this is as good as a play. Do go on."

"Where's he gone?" she said.

"If I knew I wouldn't tell you," said little Shuffle. "Good riddance, I say."

10

"But – but – he's my brother," said Mrs Well-I-Never. "He's not a good brother, but he's the only one I've got. I want him back. Where can I go to look for him?"

"You might try in the Land of Crazy People, or maybe you'd find him in the Land of Grab and Snatch, wherever that is," said Shuffle, enjoying himself. "Or possibly in the Land of Rubbish. Or—"

"Don't," said Mrs Well-I-Never, in tears. "I didn't mean to wish him away. We shall never see him again. Poor, poor Grabbit."

"Well, *I* can put up with that all right," said Shuffle cheerfully. Then he felt sorry for Mrs Well-I-Never. "Look," he said, "have you forgotten the wish that Grabbit wished?"

"Of course I haven't," said Mrs Well-I-Never. "A really silly wish – he wished I'd be sensible for once."

"Well, *be* sensible," said Shuffle. "Use your last wish and wish Grabbit back if you want him so badly. But personally I should think a few new hats would be a much better wish for you."

"Well, I never! To think I didn't think of that!" said Mrs Well-I-Never, cheering up. "Of course, I've still got a wish left. Grabbit, I wish you back!"

And back he came, frowning and furious. He had been in the Land of Rubbish and it wasn't nice.

Shuffle disappeared, grinning. Well, well, let them argue it out between them. He'd better go back and get three more wishing spells to take to Dame Dandy.

"Ma's right. She said if you gave good things to bad people they would only make bad come out of them," he said. "Scoot off, you listening rabbits, the show's over."

# She Never Could Remember

"I'm home, Mummy!" called Pam, flying into the sitting-room and flinging her school-bag on the table. "What's for lunch?"

"Something nice," said Mother. "Hang up your hat and coat and scarf. Where are your gloves? Your hands are cold."

"Oh, in my pocket, I expect!" said Pam. She felt there and then in the other pocket. But they weren't there.

"Pam! You haven't lost them again, have you?" said her mother, vexed. "It's really too bad of you. That's the third pair this month."

"Oh, dear – I can't think how it is they disappear like that," said Pam.

"Now listen," said Mother. "I shall sew a little button in each of your pockets, and sew a tape to each of your gloves. And at the other end of the tape I shall make a buttonhole, so that you can button your gloves into your pocket! Then they won't be lost."

"But the tape will show, Mummy – coming out of my pocket to my gloves," said Pam.

"Yes, it will," said Mother. "But it can't be helped. I'm not going to have you losing a fourth pair of gloves. Now go and hang up your things."

Pam's mother did as she said. She

sewed little buttons inside Pam's coat-pockets, buttoned a length of tape on to them, and sewed the gloves to the end of the tape. Now, even if Pam forgot to put them into her pocket, it didn't matter – they would hang safely down on the tapes!

Well, Pam went off to school that afternoon feeling cross. She knew the other children would tease her about the gloves on tapes, and they did. She sulked all the way home and stamped crossly into the house.

"Wipe your feet!" called her mother. "They must be very dirty on a day like this. Well – what about your gloves? Did you bring them back safely this time?"

"Yes, Mummy," said Pam, sulkily. "They're on my hands, look. I kept them on all the way home. You needn't have taped them on like that. Everyone laughed at me."

"Well, you shouldn't have been so careless, dear," said her mother. "Now hang up your things. Where's your scarf?"

Would you believe it, Pam hadn't got her scarf! There was her hat – there was her coat – and her gloves, of course – but no scarf! "I must have left it at school," she said, in a small voice.

"There now!" said her mother. "That shows how careless you are, doesn't it! Go back at once and get it."

Pam ran back and halfway there she found it lying by the roadside in the mud. Oh, dear! It must have fallen off without her knowing it. She ran back quickly, wanting her tea.

"I hadn't left it at school," she said. "It just dropped off, that's all. Here it is. A bit muddy, I'm afraid."

Her mother looked at it grimly. "A bit muddy! It's black! Very well, Pam, when it's washed and dry you can wear it again but I shall pin it to your coat in future – then it can't drop off again."

"Oh, Mummy! I can't go to school with taped gloves and a pinned-on scarf!" wailed Pam. But it wasn't a bit of good talking to her mother like that. If her mother said a thing, she meant it.

So next day off went Pam to school with her gloves taped to her pockets and her scarf pinned to her coat. It was a very warm day and she puffed and panted. How she wished she could take off her scarf, but she didn't dare to unpin it.

It was such a lovely day that the teacher let all the children out early. "Go and play in the field," said Miss Brown. "You've all worked hard this morning, and you deserve a little extra play."

So out they all went into the field.

"Let's play rounders," said John. "Come on, pick sides."

So they picked sides and then began to play. But before two minutes had gone by they were all much too hot.

"Gracious! We'll have to take off our hats and coats," said Kenneth. "Pile them over here, on this old tree-stump."

So coats and hats were quickly thrown over the old stump and the children began to play again. It was fun, in the warm autumn sun.

A bell rang suddenly. It was from the

school. "That's for the bus children!" cried John. "My word – is that the bus coming now? We'll have to hurry!"

All the bus children snatched up hats and coats and ran for the bus. Pam didn't have to catch the bus, so she didn't go with them but she suddenly remembered something.

"Gracious! Mummy told me to be sure and come home early today because we're going to see Granny's new house!" she thought. "And it's later than usual now. I must run!"

She ran to the gate, slipped through it and rushed home. She quite forgot her coat and other things. She was so warm that she didn't miss them at all.

She ran in, panting. Mother was in the kitchen serving up the lunch. She called to Pam.

"Pam, it's late, dear. Take off your things quickly and wash your hands. Bring me your gloves to let me see if they are clean enough to go to Granny's in."

Pam looked at her hands but, of course, she had no gloves on. Oh, dear – were they in her pocket then? She couldn't have lost them because they were buttoned into each pocket!

She had no pockets – because she had no coat! She stood still, quite bewildered. She put her hand up to her neck. No scarf either! Oh, goodness, what had happened?

Her mother came in, carrying a hot dish. She looked at Pam. "Did you hear me say I wanted to look at your gloves?" she said. "Where are they – in your coat pocket? My word, you have got your

things off quickly!"

"Mummy," said Pam, her face bright red, "I haven't got my gloves – or my scarf. I – I – "

"What do you mean?" said her mother, putting the dish down. "I pinned your scarf to your coat and buttoned your gloves into your pockets. Don't be silly."

Pam didn't know what to say. She was wondering about her things. Could she really have come home without them?

"Don't stand there staring, child!" said her mother sharply. "Lunch is waiting and we've got a bus to catch. Fetch your coat and get your gloves out of the pockets."

"Mummy – I haven't got my coat. I – well, I forgot it," said Pam. "And my hat, too."

Her mother stared at her in amazement. "Pam! You forgot your coat – with the scarf and gloves fastened to it – and your hat, too? How could you have forgotten them?"

"We all went to play rounders in the field and we were too hot, so we took off our things and when I ran home, because I was late, I left them behind," said poor Pam, all in a rush.

"Well you'll just have to go and get them then," said her mother. "And either you will have to go without your lunch or I shall have to go to Granny's without you. What am I to do with you? Shall I pin your hat to your head and your coat to your back?"

Pam ran off, crying. She was ashamed and upset. Now she knew how careless she was! To think she could leave everything behind!

She ran to the field. She went to the old tree-stump but it was empty except for green ivy-leaves growing all over it. Not a single coat or hat was left there!

Pam looked in horror. Some tramp must have come along and stolen it. Whatever would Mummy say now. It was a new school coat, only bought that term. Had she enough money in her money-box to buy another?

"Perhaps somebody found my things and took them to the police station," thought Pam, at last. "People are supposed to take anything they find to the police. I'll go and ask."

She was rather scared of going to the police station, but she did so hope to find her things there, so up the steps she went and walked timidly into the room where two policemen sat busily writing. They were surprised to see Pam.

Pam stammered out what she had come for. "Please – has somebody brought my things?" she said.

The bigger policeman of the two shook his head. "No. Nothing's been brought in, Miss. We'll let you know if they are. My word, that was a careless thing to do,

wasn't it – to leave the whole lot behind!"

"And you've got to remember something else, Miss," said the other policeman, solemnly. "Supposing we find that a tramp has stolen them, or somebody else that came by, and we catch him. You wouldn't like to think somebody had been sent to prison because you'd been careless enough to leave your clothes for him to steal, would you?"

This was a most alarming thought. Pam wouldn't say a word. She went home very sad indeed. As she went down the road the bus passed her – and there was Mummy in it! She had waited and waited for Pam, and hadn't been able to wait any longer.

Pam was so upset that she went down in to the back garden, sat in the fork of the old apple-tree, and cried. She'd lost her lunch and lost the treat of going to see Granny's new house – besides losing her clothes as well. She stayed out in the garden for a long time, miserable and cross with herself. Then she felt cold and went slowly indoors. A smell of burning came to her nose.

She ran into the kitchen. Oh, dear, oh, dear! Mummy had left her lunch warming up in the oven, and everything in the dish was frizzled brown! To think she could have had her lunch after all!

Then she caught sight of something very peculiar indeed – something that made her stare and stare.

Her hat and coat were hanging on their usual peg! Her scarf was there too – and her gloves peeped out of the pockets! What a very, very strange thing!

"Did I come home in them after all?" Pam thought. "Did I? I must have done. Oh, how forgetful I am! No wonder Mummy gets so cross with me. Whatever can I do to show her I'm not as bad as she thinks?"

Well, you should have seen how busy Pam was after that. She took down her mother's sewing-basket and mended

27

every pair of socks there – and mended them well, too. She went to her mother's linen-basket and pulled out hankies and vests and a blouse of her own and she washed them beautifully! Out on the line they all went.

Then she went to look in the shed. There was her father's bicycle, and her mother's too, both rather dirty. She got cloths and dusters and she cleaned those two bicycles till they shone!

She was very hungry, because she had

had no lunch. Should she get herself some tea? It was very late now – about half past five. How she wished she had been to Granny's and had one of Granny's glorious teas – a large slice of real chocolate cake, egg sandwiches, home-made ginger biscuits, and perhaps a warm jam tart! It made her feel very hungry to think of such a good tea.

She heard somebody coming in at the front door. Could it possibly be her mother, coming home so early? She flew out to see – and it was!

"I came home early because I knew you'd be all alone," said Mother. "I passed you in the bus. Did you see me?"

"Yes, Mummy!" said Pam. "I was awfully silly – I went down to the garden and cried and when I got back to the house the lunch that you left was all frizzled up, so I couldn't eat it. But, Mummy, I must have come home in my things after all, because – look, they're hanging on their usual peg!"

"Yes, I know," said Mother. "I put them there. Kind little Jane brought them home for you – and you'd just gone off to find them! You didn't hear me calling you back. Why were you gone so long?"

Pam told her about the police station. "I'm glad nobody stole my things," she said, feeling happier. "I wouldn't like to feel that somebody was in prison for stealing just because I was careless enough to leave my things in the field for them to take!"

"What's that washing on the line?" said Mother, suddenly, seeing it out of the window.

"Oh, I did want to show you I'm not as bad as you think, Mummy," said Pam, "so I did your bits of washing and I mended the socks – and I've cleaned the bicycles!"

"Well! Now I know you're better than I ever imagined!" said Mother, pleased. "And look what I've brought you from Granny!"

She opened a big paper bag and set out egg sandwiches on the table, six ginger biscuits, a most enormous slice of chocolate cake, and two little jam tarts.

"Dear old Granny sent them for you,"
she said. "I said no, I wasn't going to
take anything home to such a careless,
naughty girl, but Granny said I might
find a good one when I got in – and she
was right!"

Pam was so pleased. She sat down and
began to eat hungrily. "Listen, Mummy,"

31

she said, when she had finished, "You don't need to pin my scarf on any more, or tape my gloves to my pockets. I've turned over a new leaf – a huge new leaf – and you can trust me now!"

And her mother at once unpinned the scarf and snipped the tape of the gloves. Wasn't that nice of her? She felt sure that Pam was telling the truth.

She was, of course. She's the most dependable little girl you ever saw now!

# The
# Blow-Abouts

It was a very windy day – so windy that all the trees were bent over, and all the grasses sang a little whistling song. Mollie and John were hurrying home from school, and the wind played them all sorts of tricks as they went.

First it blew John's book away, and sent it flying along the grass. Then it took Mollie's hat right off her head. Every time Mollie bent down to pick it up the wind blew it a little further off again, and really, it seemed exactly as if it was playing with her.

Suddenly Mollie stopped, and pointed up in the air.

"Look, John!" she cried. "Whatever's that coming down from the sky?"

John looked.

"It looks like a crowd of little people hanging on to a big toy balloon!" he said. "What a peculiar thing!"

Sure enough, it was! The big blue balloon came quickly downwards, and hanging on to its string were four small people that looked rather like pixie-folk. They rolled over and over on the ground as the balloon came to earth. Then they picked themselves up and dusted their coats.

"Here's a fine thing!" said the biggest one. "Now what are we to do?"

"What's the matter?" asked John, running up. "Do you always go about on the string of a balloon?"

"Yes, because we are the Blow-Abouts. Didn't you know?" said the biggest one. "We're always blowing about somewhere. But our balloon is gradually getting smaller. Look at it – the poor thing has almost gone to nothing now. There must be a leak in it somewhere, for it was quite all right when we started out this morning."

"Where are we?" asked the smallest

Blow-About. "I suppose this is part of Fairyland, isn't it?"

"No, it's the place where men and women and boys and girls live," said Mollie. "Have you come from Fairyland?"

"No, from Dreamland," answered the Blow-About. "We were on our way to Fairyland, you know. I suppose the wind must have blown us out of our way – it's in a very mischievous mood this morning, isn't it?"

"How are we to get back?" asked the biggest Blow-About. "We really must get to Fairyland tonight, you know. We promised to sing at the Queen's party."

"Well, our balloon is busted," said the littlest one.

"You shouldn't say 'busted', you should say 'bursted'," said the biggest one.

"But that's not right either," said John.

"Don't argue," said all the Blow-Abouts at once. "Can't you advise us how to get back?"

"No," said John, thinking hard, "I can't. I haven't a balloon and my toy aeroplane is broken – and – oh, I know!"

"What!" cried Mollie and the Blow-Abouts together.

"There's my umbrella that blew inside out yesterday," said John. "Could we use that, somehow, do you think?"

"The very thing!" cried the biggest Blow-About. "We'll go with you, and see it." So all six of them ran off together, and John fetched his broken umbrella from the playroom and showed it to the Blow-bouts. The biggest Blow-About looked at it and frowned. Then he suddenly clapped his hands.

"I've got it!" he cried. "We'll make a kind of parachute! Quick! Help me to take out this stick!"

Together they worked the stick of the umbrella out. They had to cut it at the end, and soon the umbrella looked very peculiar.

"Get a big curtain ring and some strong string," commanded the biggest Blow-About, getting very hot as he worked.

Mollie found a curtain ring, and John brought some string.

"Thanks," said the Blow-About. He cut the string into equal pieces, and tied each piece to a point of the umbrella. Then he tied all the other ends of the string to the curtain ring.

"Now there's a fine parachute!" he cried. "All it wants is the wind to blow it along! Come along now, and maybe we'll catch the five o'clock breeze!"

"The five o'clock breeze!" cried Mollie. "I didn't know there were winds like that!"

"You don't know much!" said the

biggest Blow-About, cheekily. "You have five o'clock buses and trains and things, don't you? Well, we have winds that run to time, too, and take us where we want to go!"

"How are we all going to get on to the parachute?" asked the littlest Blow-About, anxiously. "There's only one curtain ring to hold on to, you know!"

"We'll manage somehow!" said the biggest one. He caught hold of the ring and held on as the wind filled the parachute and lifted it. "Catch hold of my legs, one of you! Here comes the wind!"

One of the Blow-Abouts did so and then the next took hold of the second one's feet. The littlest one of all, who was really hardly any weight, caught hold of the third one – and then off they went into the air on the five o'clock wind!

Up they went, up and up, while Mollie and John shouted in delight.

"Thanks very much!" cried the Blow-Abouts. "This is ever so much better than a balloon! We shall always use your old umbrella, John."

And as far as I know, they always have. They sometimes come blowing over our land on a moonlight night, so you must watch out for them. Mollie and John have only seen them once more, and then they noticed that their old umbrella was painted in very bright colours. So, as John said, "It's just as well not to throw anything away because you never know when Blow-Abouts or someone like them will come along and use it!"

# It Happened
## One Afternoon

Mike went whistling into his father's study to borrow a map. He and his friend Joe were going on a weekend bicycle tour, and Mike wanted to work out the best way to go.

Mike felt happy. It was a wonderful day, and looked like being a wonderful weekend. He and Joe were to go off that evening, after Joe had finished at the office he worked at. He was sixteen, and very anxious to get on. Mike was almost fifteen and still at school.

It was half-term. His bicycle was cleaned, ready for the weekend. His mother had already packed him up a bag of food. His father had given him some money to spend on himself and Joe over the weekend. Everything was fine.

He found the map and slipped it into his pocket. Then he caught sight of a new golf club that his father had bought himself. It stood by the desk, neat and shining.

"Ha! Dad's got a new club!" said Mike and he picked it up. "I bet I could hit a golf ball as far as he can. Wheeeeee!"

He swung it up behind him and brought it down. *Crash*!

Mike turned in fright. He had smashed a lamp and a very valuable vase. Broken pieces of them lay all over the desk and floor.

Mike did the first thing he thought of. He shot out of the room, down the passage to the garden door and out to the shed. He hid there, trembling.

"Dad would be furious if he thought I'd done that," he thought. "So would Mum. They wouldn't let me go away for the weekend with Joe. I wouldn't be surprised if Dad stopped my pocket money."

He stayed there for a long while. He could hear excited voices, and knew that the breakages had been discovered. He wondered what to do.

He didn't think of owning up and facing up to his punishment. Let them think it was the cat! Tabitha was always breaking something.

He stayed in the shed till teatime. He knew his mother would have gone out by then to see his grandmother. Dad didn't seem to be about either – maybe he wasn't home yet. He wouldn't bother about tea. He would just scribble a note to say he was sorry they were out when he set off for his weekend.

"I don't want to face them so soon after the things got broken," he thought. "I'll just let them think I couldn't say goodbye because they weren't here when I left – and by Monday perhaps they'll have forgotten all about the accident, and won't ask any awkward questions."

He scribbled his note, crept out and snooped around to see where everyone was.

"No sign of Mum, and no sign of Dad either," he thought. "Good. I'll leave the note on Mum's chair. She'll see it when she comes back."

He left the note, jumped on his bicycle and rode off down the path and into the lane to go to Joe's. His rucksack was on his back, with the things in it he would need. Joe was bringing some, too. It would be fun!

He rode in at the gate at the bottom of Joe's garden. He gave the whistle that he

and Joe used but Joe didn't seem to be
there.

"Blow! There's his bike, all ready –
where on earth is Joe?"

He heard a movement in the little
summerhouse nearby, and then a scared
and anxious face looked out at him. It
was Joe's sister, twelve-year-old Jane.

"Jane! What's the matter?" asked
Mike at once. "You're crying. What's
happened? Is somebody ill?"

"No," said Jane, with a gulp. "Oh,
Mike! It's awful!"

"What's awful?" said Mike, going into
the summerhouse, feeling very worried.

He was fond of Jane. "Have you gone and got yourself into trouble, Jane? What have you done? Lost your homework again?"

"No, Mike – nothing like that. It's poor Joe," said Jane, and began to cry again.

"What's happened to him?" asked Mike, impatiently. "He ought to be here, ready to start out with me. Don't say something's happened to stop him!"

"He's not coming," said Jane, almost in a whisper. "He's in awful trouble. He's lost his job at Mr Frost's office. Dad's furious with him."

"Gosh – but what's he *done*?" asked Mike. "Do tell me, Jane. This is awful."

"I don't know exactly what he's done, nor where it all happened," said Jane. "They wouldn't let me be in the room. All I know is that Joe was sent out to deliver some important papers from the office this afternoon – and – and they say he went to deliver them – climbed in at the window because he saw a gold watch there – and stole it!"

Mike listened, absolutely amazed. *Joe*!

Why, Joe was as honest as the day. "It can't be true," he said at last. "It's a wicked thing to say about Joe!"

"Yes, I know," said Jane, wiping away her tears. "But he was found standing in the room and the watch was gone. They think he must have thrown it out of the window as soon as he heard someone coming. That's what they say."

"But they must be mad," said Mike. "Joe couldn't do a thing like that! He simply couldn't. He must have been in the room for some quite good reason. I know Joe!"

"Joe said he heard a peculiar noise and jumped in to see what it was," said Jane. "They didn't believe him, of course."

"Look here!" said Mike, feeling very fierce all of a sudden. "I'm going to find out where this place is that Joe's supposed to have stolen the watch from. I'm going to go and see these horrible people there. I'm going to tell them that Joe's my friend and couldn't do a mean thing to save his life! See, Jane?"

"Oh, Mike!" said Jane, looking at him with the greatest admiration. "Would you really be brave enough to do all that? You would be a good friend to Joe!"

"He's my best friend and I won't let anyone treat him like that or say things like that about him!" said Mike. "What's more, when I've seen these people and told them what I think of them, I shall go and see your father and mother, and tell them they ought to know better than to think old Joe would ever do such a thing as steal a gold watch and tell lies about it!"

He got up and Jane got up, too, drying her eyes. "Perhaps they'll let you and Joe go off for the weekend after all," she said. "Oh, Mike – I do think you are wonderful."

"Where's Joe?" said Mike. "Come on, let's find him."

Joe was in his room, sulky and miserable. Mike went up to him and thumped him on the back.

"Cheer up, old chap! I'll go and face these people who say things like that about you! Tell me all about it."

"Haven't you heard all about it?" asked Joe, looking suddenly astonished.

"Well – only what Jane's told me," said Mike. Joe went on looking astonished, and didn't say a word. "Do tell me what happened," said Mike. "I want to know so that I can march straight off to these people and tell them what I think of them."

Joe looked at Mike doubtfully. "Well – it seems odd that you haven't heard all about it yet," he said. "I'll tell you exactly what happened. I was told to take some important papers to a client this afternoon. So off I went. Well, as I passed a window as I was walking up to the front door, I suddenly heard a most terrific crash! I nearly jumped out of my skin. I looked in at the open window and saw a frightful mess on the floor."

"What was it?" asked Mike.

"I don't really know," said Joe. "Anyway, I stood there wondering what had caused all the noise and mess and thought I'd better investigate. So I jumped in at the window – but I hadn't been there more than a moment before in came the client, and shouted at me to know what I was doing there, and what had I smashed!"

"Go on," said Mike. "What beastly people!"

"I was just explaining that I'd jumped in merely to see what was happening when his wife called out that a gold watch was missing – it had been left on the desk and it wasn't there. So they

thought I'd taken it – got in at the window, you see, knocked over a heap of things, and then got frightened and chucked the watch away."

"I call this all absolute rubbish!" said Mike, fiercely. "If they knew you they'd never say things like that about you, Joe."

"Actually, they *did* know me," said Joe. "But it didn't make any difference. They rang up Mr Frost and told him what they thought I'd done, and when I got back to the office he was very angry at my behaviour and sacked me – gave me my money and sent me off straight away. My father's furious."

"I'm going to see these hateful people," said Mike. "Who are they? Tell me their name and address, Joe."

Joe didn't say anything. He went very red and looked at the floor.

"Go on, Joe – tell me quickly," said Mike.

"Mike," said Joe in a low voice, "it – it was your house and your family. You see, I thought I knew you well enough to leap

in at the window to see if anything was going wrong – I didn't realise they'd think I'd smashed those things and taken the watch."

Mike sat down suddenly. He stared at Joe. A horrid sick feeling came over him, and thoughts raced through his mind. He knew at once what had happened!

Joe had just been passing his house when he, Mike, had smashed the vase and the lamp with his father's golf club. Joe had leaped in to see what the noise was – and had found nobody there, because Mike had run straight out of the room and hidden. The gold watch? Yes, it had been there all right but probably Mike had hit that, too, and quite likely it was in some dark corner of the room, smashed to bits.

He sat staring at Joe, feeling wicked and very miserable. Joe had been punished for something he, Mike, had done and had run away from. Joe had lost his job. Joe was in disgrace. Their weekend was ruined. What was to be done?

"You see – you won't go and face those people now," said Joe miserably. "They're your own people. They wouldn't believe even you!"

Mike stood up, very pale. "They *will* believe me," he said. "And you'll get your job back, and your father will be very sorry he scolded you. You'll see! But we shan't go off for our weekend. And shall I tell you why? It's because you'll never want to see me again after today!"

He went off, leaving Jane and Joe very

surprised and puzzled. He knew what he had to do. He had to do the thing he had run away from that afternoon. He had to go and own up and take his punishment.

He went straight home and found his father. "Dad," he said, "ring up Mr Frost and tell him to take Joe back at once. I'm the one to blame."

"Now, what exactly do you mean, Mike?" said his father, astonished.

Mike told him. "I came in here and saw your new golf club. I swung it – and smashed the lamp and the vase. And I was a coward and ran off to hide in the shed. I hoped Mum would think it was the cat who had broken the things. I didn't know Joe was going to be blamed."

His father listened in silence, his face very grave. "What about the gold watch?" he said. "That's missing, as you know."

"It's probably lying in the grate or under the bookcase, smashed," said Mike. "I may have hit that too and sent it flying. I'll look, Dad."

He looked – and sure enough the watch was under the bookcase, badly damaged. He laid it in front of his father in silence.

"Punish me twice," said Mike. "Once for doing all this and once for making the blame fall on someone else. I know I'm a coward and you're ashamed of me. I'm ashamed of myself. I know I've lost your good opinion, and I shall have lost Mum's trust – and I've certainly lost Joe's friendship. I'm a – a worm."

"Yes. I rather think you are," said his father. "The only good thing in the whole affair is that you owned up when you saw that Joe was being punished. I'm disappointed in you. Horribly disappointed. It will take you a long while to get back my trust and make me proud of you – and your mother will think the same. Now go away and ask your mother to come to me."

Mike was in for a very bad time indeed. His father would hardly speak to him. His mother looked as if she was going to burst into tears each time she looked at him. Mr Frost turned the other way when he met him.

But would you believe it, Joe didn't turn against him! He was just the same as usual, friendly, kind and generous.

"Ass!" he said, when Mike thanked him for being so decent. "Aren't I your friend? You're in trouble and you want help. All right, that's what a friend is for. Come on, we'll face this together, and when everyone sees us about as usual, they'll soon forget what's happened! You were a coward – but you were jolly brave, too, to go and own up just for me!"

Things will work out all right, of course, but what a good thing for Mike that he had a friend like Joe! I'd like to be as good a friend as that, wouldn't you?

# A Surprise
# for Bimbo

One day Bimbo, the naughty Siamese kitten, went creeping into the kitchen to see if there was anything he could eat. Sometimes his mistress dropped things on the floor, and if she couldn't stop to pick them up at that moment, there was just a chance that he could snap them up!

"Mistress dropped a bit of bacon rind yesterday," thought Bimbo. "And once she dropped a sausage! Maybe she will drop a haddock today, or something really exciting!"

So he sat patiently under the table and waited and waited. But all that his mistress dropped was a fork that stuck into Bimbo's tail, and he didn't like that at all!

He was just going away when his

mistress went to answer the door. Bimbo jumped up on to the table at once. Mistress was making cakes, but there was nothing there for Bimbo to eat. He didn't want flour. He didn't want sugar. He didn't want currants.

But wait a minute, what was this? There was a little jug of milk on the table, and oh, the cream on the top of that milk!

"Now this is something worth having!" thought Bimbo in delight, and he put his head down to the jug. He put out his pink tongue, but alas, it couldn't reach the cream because the jug was only half full.

"Well, there's nothing for it but to put my head into the jug and lick the milk like that," thought Bimbo. He took a quick look up the hallway. Good, Mistress was still talking at the door. So into the neck of the jug went Bimbo's little head, and he began to lick up the cream greedily.

Then he heard his mistress close the door and he knew she was coming back.

What a scolding he would get if she found him stealing the milk. He tried to take his head out of the jug at once, but he couldn't! It was stuck!

He tried and tried. He heard his mistress coming back into the kitchen. Poor Bimbo! He jumped down from the table with his head still in the jug. Milk poured all over him!

He ran quickly out of the door, banging himself on the side of it as he went, because, of course, he couldn't see with his head inside the jug!

Down the passageway he ran, and came to the little room where his mistress often worked. He thought he would go in there and work the jug off his head in peace. He slipped inside the room and sat down, panting, the jug still over his head. It was hard to breathe properly with it on, and it felt very tight and uncomfortable.

"The milk has soaked my face," thought Bimbo. "It is perfectly horrid. I don't like it at all. I am very unhappy. Now, before anyone comes, I really *must* try to drag this jug off my head. My front paws will help me."

So Bimbo sat and tried to pull the jug off his head with his paws. But it simply wouldn't come!

"Bones and biscuits, tails and whiskers, whatever in the world am I to do?" thought poor Bimbo, in a fright. "Have I got to wear this jug all the rest of my life? I do hope not. I'd better go and find Topsy and see if she will pull it off for me."

So off he went out of the little room to

find Topsy. He couldn't see at all where he was going, and he kept bumping into the wall and making a tremendous noise.

*Bang-bang*, *bang-crash*, he went. Topsy, the little fox-terrier puppy, heard the strange noise and pricked up her ears. She ran to see what it was. Bimbo heard the pitter-patter of her paws and called out to Topsy. "Topsy, help me! Topsy, help me!"

But the jug made his voice sound very odd indeed, just like yours sounds when

you roll up a newspaper and then talk down it. "Wop-wop-wop-wop!" his voice sounded like. "Wop-wop-wop-wop!"

Topsy stared and listened in the greatest astonishment. What could this creature be with a jug for a head and a voice that said "Wop-wop-wop-wop!" all the time? Topsy didn't like it. She put her tail down and fled away to find the other animals, Bobs the black-and-white fox terrier and Cosy the tabby cat.

Bimbo clattered after her, the jug bumping against the walls as he ran. Topsy found Bobs and Cosy and wuffed to them.

"There's a jug-headed animal in the house that says 'Wop-wop-wop-wop!' in a funny deep voice. I'm frightened! Save me!"

"Don't be silly," said Bobs, getting up. "A jug-headed animal with a voice that says 'Wop-wop-wop-wop!' You must be mad!"

But when Bimbo came round the corner with the jug still on his head,

crying for help in a voice that still sounded exactly like "Wop-wop-wop!" all the three animals were as scared as could be. They fled into the garden at once. And out into the garden after them went Bimbo, crying for help. It was a strange sight to see.

Goodness knows what would have happened if Bimbo hadn't run straight into the wall. The jug broke in half and fell off, and there was Bimbo's face looking at the others, scared and soaked with milk.

"Bimbo! Is this a new game or something?" cried Bobs. "Whatever did you put a jug on your head for? You gave us an awful fright."

"I didn't put it on," said poor Bimbo, beginning to wash his face clean. "It wouldn't come off, that's all. And I think you are a lot of mean creatures, running away when I kept calling out for help."

"Well, we *would* have helped you if only you had said something sensible instead of 'Wop-wop-wop-wop!'" said Topsy. "We couldn't think what that meant, so we ran away."

"I did *not* say 'Wop-wop-wop-wop!'" said Bimbo. "But maybe the jug over my head made my words sound like that. You go and get a jug over your head and talk down it, and see what it sounds like, one of you."

But nobody wanted to, and don't you try either, will you!

# Tip, Top
# and Tup

There were once three bold tinkers of Fairyland called Tip, Top and Tup. They went round doing odd jobs, such as grinding scissors, glueing broken pots and mending chairs. They were cheeky and merry, always singing songs and laughing.

> Hey, good people, come to us,
> We'll mend your chairs for you,
> We'll grind your scissors
>    nice and sharp,
> And mend your crocks with glue.

So they went along singing and whistling, while people came running out with things for Tip, Top and Tup to mend.

Now one day they came to a town where many people were gathered in the market-place, all talking at once.

"Hey, good folk, what is all this to-do?" called Tip.

"Oh, haven't you heard?" cried an old market woman. "There's been an earthquake quite near here, and the Lord High Chancellor's palace got a terrible shaking!"

"Did it indeed?" said Top. "Did it fall down?"

"Oh, no," said the woman. "But nearly everything in the palace is broken."

"Broken!" said Tup, staring at Tip.

"Broken!" said Tip, staring at Top.

"Broken!" said Top, staring at Tup. "Then that's the place for us! We shall make our fortunes in mending the things in the Lord High Chancellor's palace!"

They took hands and went dancing off down the street, singing at the tops of their voices:

> Three tinkers we,
> Oh, tiddley-tee!

What wonderful things we'll do
In the palace high!
Pi, tiddley-ti!
With our marvellous pots of glue!

"You won't get paid much!" shouted a gnome after them.

"Why not?" shouted the tinkers.

"Because the Chancellor's the meanest man in the kingdom. He won't even blow on his porridge in case he wastes his breath!"

"Ho, ho! He, he!" laughed Tip, Top and Tup, dancing out of sight.

They went to the palace that stood on the hill in the distance. It was really very beautiful, but it certainly looked as if an earthquake had passed that way, for most of the windows were broken, and one or two chimneys looked rather odd.

Tip, Top and Tup went round to the back door and knocked loudly. A scullery maid opened it. Tip, Top and Tup bowed low and swept the floor with their feathered hats.

"We are tinkers," said Tip. "Is there work for us to do here?"

"Dear me, I should think so!" said the scullery maid. "Come in, and I'll see if the Lord High Chancellor will see you."

The tinkers wiped their feet carefully on the mat and stepped inside. The scullery maid told the cook about them, the cook told the butler, and the butler told a footman. The footman went to the Lord Chancellor and told him.

"Humph!" said the Chancellor. "Bring them in."

Tip, Top and Tup walked into the great room where the Chancellor was sitting. They bowed, marched forward, clicked their heels together, and smiled their best smiles.

Said Tip: "If you've dishes to mend,"

Said Top: "Or odd jobs to do,"

Said Tup: "Just leave them to us,"

Said Tip: "For we've gallons of glue!"

"Humph!" said the Chancellor. "There are plenty of odd jobs about the palace, because an earthquake upset us all yesterday. You can stay here and do them.

71

But, mind, they must be done well, or I'll turn you out, neck and crop!"

"What is a crop?" asked Tip.

"Humph!" said the Chancellor. "Fancy not knowing that! You'd better go back to school again!"

"But what is it?" asked Top.

The Chancellor didn't know, so he couldn't say. "Stop these silly questions!" he said. "Go and start your work at once!" Off went the three tinkers, swinging their pots of glue.

They went all over the palace first of all, to see exactly what was broken and to decide what they had better start on first.

They spent one hour looking round, and then sat down to talk.

"Fifty-three chairs to mend," said Tip.

"Thirty-one pictures to mend," said Top.

"Sixty-nine dishes to mend," said Tup.

"And two hundred and forty-one cups and saucers," said Tip.

They got up and did a little dance of joy and sang loudly:

> This will make our fortunes,
> There isn't any doubt,
> For never, never have we seen
> So many jobs about!

Then they rushed off and began to mend all the broken things. Tip did the chairs, Top did the pictures and Tup did the dishes. It took them a long time, but they did it well, and made the glue extra strong in case another earthquake came along.

Everybody in the palace liked having them there, for they were so merry and so jolly. Only the Chancellor disliked them, because he didn't think they were as respectful to him as they ought to be, and they had an annoying habit of singing at him in rhyme. He wasn't clever enough to answer back in rhyme, so he simply scowled at them and said "Humph!" a great many times.

When they met him in the palace they would line up against the wall, salute very smartly, and sing:

Good morning,
    Lord High Chancellor.
Did you sleep well last night?
And do you bring to all your meals
A healthy appetite?

"Humph!" said the Chancellor, and passed them quickly.

Tip made up another little song, and sang it to all the kitchen folk.

"Humph!" he says in the morning,
and "Humph!" in the afternoon,
"Humph!" he says when
    evening comes,
And "Humph!" by the light
    of the moon.

Everybody thought it was very funny, and soon it was being hummed all over the palace.

The Chancellor heard it one day, and was very angry.

"I shan't pay those cheeky little tinkers a single penny piece!" he vowed. "Not a single penny piece!"

In four weeks' time the tinkers had finished their jobs, and there was nothing left for them to do. They had mended and glued together hundreds of things, and the palace was once again in good working order.

"Now we'll go and ask for our wages," said Tip.

"We've earned a lot of money," said Top.

"At least a hundred pounds," said Tup.

So they went in to see the Lord High Chancellor, and bowed politely.

Said Tip: "We've finished our jobs,"

Said Top: "And we've come to say,"

Said Tup: "That we'd be very glad,"

Said Tip: "If you'd give us our pay!"

"Humph!" said the Chancellor. "I shan't give you a penny!"

"What!" cried the tinkers, nearly falling over in astonishment. "But you owe us one hundred pounds!"

"One hundred, fiddlesticks!" said the Chancellor. "Be off with you! You've had food and a bed for four weeks, and that's enough pay for you. You're three cheeky

tinkers, and I want nothing more to do
with you!"

"But, sir—" said Tip, coming forward.

"I said 'Be off!'," said the Chancellor.
"If you stay here another moment I'll
ring for my soldiers and have you thrown
out of my palace!"

Tip, Top and Tup went out of the room at once. When they had got safely to the kitchen they looked at each other in dismay.

"Not a penny!" said Tip.

"And we've worked so hard!" said Top.

"Let's break everything we've mended!" said Tup.

"No, no!" said Tip. "Two wrongs don't make a right. But we must certainly punish the Chancellor somehow!"

"Let's all think how," said Top.

So they all sat down and thought hard.

"I know what I'm going to do," said Tip.

"So do I," said Top.

"And so do I," said Tup.

"I'm going to put glue on to the handle of his teapot," said Tip giggling, "and when he pours out his tea tomorrow he won't be able to let go his hold of the handle!"

"Ha, ha!" said Top. "I'm going to put glue on the front doormat, and when he wants to go out he'll find he can't, because his feet are stuck tight!"

"He, he!" said Top. "And I'm going to put glue inside his best hat so that he won't be able to take it off once he puts it on!"

"Ho, ho!" Tip laughed. "That will teach him to be mean and selfish!"

"We'll hide somewhere in the palace so that we can see the fun!" said Tip, mixing his glue.

The three rascally tinkers made the strongest glue they could, and then waited until morning came. Then Tip slipped down to the breakfast-room and put glue on the teapot handle, as soon as

he saw that the tea was made. Top spread glue on the front doormat, and Tup peeped into the Chancellor's big hatbox and spread glue round the inside of his best hat.

The Chancellor went down to breakfast. There was a letter lying on his plate and he opened it. Tip, Top and Tup were hidden behind the curtains, waiting for the fun.

"Humph!" said the Chancellor, reading his letter out loud. "'Their Majesties, the King and Queen of Fairyland, will visit your palace this afternoon and will stay to tea.' Dear me! what a very great honour! Humph!"

He picked up the teapot to pour himself out a cup of tea. He did so and set it down again, but he couldn't leave go! His hand was stuck fast!

"What an extraordinary thing!" said the Lord High Chancellor. "I can't take my hand from the teapot. I must be bewitched!"

He tried and tried, but Tip's glue was far too strong. He swung the teapot in the air and tried to shake it off, but it was no use. All that happened was that the teapot steadily poured out hot tea, and the Chancellor got scalded on one of his big toes, and danced about yelling and shouting.

The butler came rushing in, followed by the footman, and stared in surprise at his master leaping about pouring tea all over the place from the teapot!

"Your Excellency!" he cried. "The new carpet! You are spoiling it!"

"Spoiling the carpet!" yelled the Chancellor. "I've spoiled my toe – that's what I've done! I can't get rid of this teapot!"

Tip, Top and Tup laughed until the curtains shook but nobody heard or noticed, for everyone was trying to get the teapot out of the Chancellor's hand.

"Oh!" he shouted. "You're hurting me! Get away, all of you!"

Then the palace doctor came, but he couldn't do anything either and the poor Chancellor had to finish his breakfast with his right hand still holding on to the teapot, and all the morning he had to take it with him wherever he went.

"And the King and Queen are coming!" he groaned. "Whatever will they think of me if I meet them carrying a teapot! It really is a most extraordinary thing!"

He went to the front door to tell his soldiers there what to do when they saw the royal carriage arriving. He stood on the mat and gave them their orders, then turned to go. But he couldn't lift his feet up – they were stuck to the mat! Try as

he might, he couldn't move a step!
"What's happened?" he cried. "I can't
move my feet!"

The soldiers looked on with gaping
mouths, while the Chancellor tried to
lift up first one foot and then the other.

"Take your boots off, Your Excellency,"
said one of the soldiers.

The Chancellor was just going to, when he remembered that he had a large hole in one of his socks. It would never do to let his soldiers see that. How shocked they would be!

So there was nothing for it but for the Chancellor to give a jump and take the mat with him up to his bedroom. It was terribly awkward, especially up the stairs, but somehow he managed it.

How everybody stared to see the solemn Lord Chancellor jumping along the palace with a mat stuck to both his feet and a teapot in his hand! They couldn't make it out at all. As for Tip, Top and Tup, they could hardly speak for laughing.

The Chancellor slipped off his boots in his bedroom and put on another pair. Then, as it was getting near the time for the arrival of the King and Queen, he put on his best hat.

He went down to the front door, trying to look as if it was the right thing to carry a teapot about. Just as he got there the royal carriage drove up and out stepped the King and Queen.

Everybody took off his hat and waved it – all except the poor Chancellor, who couldn't get his hat off at all. It was stuck tight to his wig. He tugged and he pulled, but it wasn't a bit of use – not a bit; his hat wouldn't come off.

The King and Queen bowed to everyone and walked slowly up the steps to where the poor Chancellor stood.

The King looked at him in surprise, for he still had the teapot in his hand and his hat still on his head.

"He must be mad!" thought the King. He followed the Chancellor into the palace, taking the Queen by the hand.

The Chancellor still had his hat on, even when they reached the big hall and the King and Queen sat down on the thrones prepared for them. At last the King spoke to him.

"Take off your hat, Sir Chancellor!"

"I c-c-can't, Your Majesty!" stammered the Chancellor. "I'm under a spell, I think. This morning I couldn't let go the handle of the teapot; this afternoon I couldn't take my feet off the mat, and now I can't take my hat off my head."

Everybody was giggling, for the poor Chancellor looked so funny. The King stepped up to him and looked closely at the hat.

"There's no magic spell here!" he said. "There's glue!"

"Glue!" cried everyone, in amazement.

"Glue!" cried the Chancellor, angrily.

"Yes, glue," said the King.

"It's Tip, Top and Tup!" cried the Chancellor. "They've played this trick on me. Find them, soldiers!"

In two shakes of a dog's tail Tip, Top and Tup were found and brought before the King.

"What's the meaning of this scandalous trick?" demanded the King.

The tinkers didn't know what "scandalous" meant, but they shivered when they heard the King's angry voice.

"Please, it's because the Chancellor wouldn't pay us even a penny after we had been here for four weeks and mended up everything in the palace!" said Tip.

"Is this true?" the King asked the Chancellor.

"Yes," said he, blushing very red.

"Then you deserved to be punished," said the King. He turned to the tinkers. "But you had no right to punish him in this way. You know perfectly well you should have come to me and made your complaint, and then I should have made

the Chancellor pay you. As it is, you have lost your money and done something very silly."

"We beg your pardon, Your Majesty," said the tinkers, sorrowfully.

"I will give you work to do, and you shall be paid," said the King. "I can't trust you to find jobs yourself, for you might play even worse tricks on better men than the Chancellor."

"Yes, Your Majesty," said the tinkers, obediently.

"Go to all the chestnut trees," said the King, "and take your glue with you. The leaves are off the branches now, and the little new buds feel cold with the frost and the wind. Paint them all with your sticky glue, and that will be like a mackintosh for them, and they will no longer feel cold."

"Your Majesty, we go!" cried the tinkers. And off they went, leaving the angry Chancellor staring at them with the teapot still in his hand.

And if you feel a chestnut bud this springtime you will find that what I have said is true. Each bud is covered with the stickiest of sticky glues. So I should think Tip, Top and Tup have been very busy – wouldn't you?

# Do-as-
# You're-Told!

There was once a little boy called Jimmy, who was really a little pickle! He simply would not do as he was told.

If he was told to walk on the pavement, not in the road, he would walk a few steps and then slip off into the gutter again. And his mother would say, "Do as you're told, Jimmy."

If his father said to him, "Jimmy, sit up straight; don't loll like that," he would sit up for half a minute and then loll forward again. And his father would say, "Will you do as you're told."

So all day long Jimmy heard the same thing, "Do as you're told." But he never did. His friends called him "Do-as-you're-told" because that is what they always heard when they were with Jimmy.

"Hello, here comes old Do-as-you're-told!" they would say. "Come on, Do-as-you're-told. What shall we play today?"

And you may be sure that Do-as-you're-told would choose something he had been told not to do! Well, you can't go on like that for ever, and the day came when Jimmy got a shock.

It was a beautiful winter's day, but very, very cold. All the puddles in the road were thick ice. The duck-pond was frozen too, and so was the village pond. The boys slid on the puddles, but they were not quite sure about the ponds. They ran to school, shouting and laughing that morning, sliding on the puddles and gathering the white frost from the top of the posts.

When it was time to go home from morning school, their teacher spoke to them.

"No sliding on the duck-pond or the village pond yet," he said. "They are not safe. They may be safe tomorrow. Now, you hear me, all of you, don't you?"

## Do-as-You're-Told!

"Yes, sir!" said the boys, and they trooped out into the frosty, sunny street, shouting and running.

"I say!" said Jimmy, as they came to the big village pond. "Look at that shining ice! It's as safe as can be! Mr Brown is wrong."

"No, you do as you're told, old Do-as-you're-told!" The boys laughed, pulling Jimmy away. But he shook himself free and gazed longingly at the frozen pond.

"Wouldn't I love a good slide over the ice!" he said. "It feels so good! Whizzzzzz!

And away we go, just as if we had wings on our feet. I think I'll try it and see if it's safe. I'm pretty sure it is."

"Don't, Jimmy," said the biggest boy. "You know what Mr Brown said."

"Well, it's too bad," said Jimmy. "I've been looking forward to sliding on this pond all the morning. And now he says we're not to! That means no sliding today – and tomorrow the weather might be warmer and the ice will melt! We shall have missed our sliding!"

"Oh, come home!" said the boys. "It's dinner-time."

But Jimmy wouldn't move. He simply longed to go sliding. Silly old Mr Brown to say the pond wasn't safe! Why, the ice was as thick as could be! Jimmy put his foot on it to try it. It didn't crack at all. He put his other foot on it, and stood with all his weight there. No cracks!

"It's safe, I tell you!" said Jimmy, in delight. "Watch me slide!"

He set off over the frozen pond, he slid a lovely long way, and then, alas, he came to a thin piece! The ice cracked under

his weight. It made a noise like the sound of a whip being cracked in the air.

"Oh! Oh!" cried Jimmy, in fright. He tried to stop himself sliding but he couldn't. He slid on and fell right into the water that came pouring through the cracks in the ice. He went down into the pond. It was icy cold – oh, so icy, icy cold!

Poor Jimmy! He tried to catch hold of the sides of the ice, but it was dreadfully slippery. He yelled for help. He was wet through, and the water was the coldest he had ever felt. Even his teeth began to shiver.

The watching boys were scared. The biggest one ran to the carpenter's shop nearby, shouting for a ladder. The carpenter picked one up and ran to the pond. He placed the ladder flat down on the ice and pushed it carefully towards Jimmy, who was still trying to catch hold of the edges of the ice. Nearer and nearer slid the ladder, and at last it reached Jimmy. He caught hold of the nearest rung, and then the carpenter pulled hard at the ladder. Jimmy was drawn right out of the water.

He began to clamber over the flat ladder, shivering and weeping.

The carpenter took him into his house, stripped off his wet clothes and dried him in front of a big fire. Jimmy was very frightened indeed. He couldn't stop shivering.

"Well, Do-as-you're-told, see what's happened to you!" said the carpenter, as he rubbed Jimmy dry. "I suppose you thought you knew better than Mr Brown! Now you run home in this old suit of mine and tell your mother what's happened."

Off ran Jimmy, looking very strange in the kind carpenter's big suit. When his mother heard what had happened she put him straight to bed, for she was afraid he would get a bad cold.

Two of the boys came to see Jimmy that afternoon, after school. "What lessons did you do?" asked Jimmy, sitting up in bed.

"We didn't do any," said Harry. "Mr Brown took us up into the hills, where that old sheep-pond is. It's much colder there than here and the sheep-pond is frozen fast. We've been sliding all the afternoon! My goodness, Jimmy, we did have fun! You ought to have been there! The ice was as thick as could be!"

"We're going again tomorrow afternoon," said George, the other boy. "Perhaps you can come too, if you're all right, Jimmy."

But Jimmy wasn't all right. He had caught a very bad cold and his mother kept him in bed for a week. And by the time he got up, the ice had gone! The weather had turned warm and not a single pond was frozen.

Jimmy was very unhappy. He had had a dreadful shock and caught a horrible cold – *and* missed all the fun of sliding up in the hills. He turned his face into his pillow and cried, for he felt rather small and miserable.

"I shan't disobey again," he thought. "Nobody punished me for it – but I punished myself, and it was a dreadful punishment!"

Now nobody calls him Do-as-you're-told. He is just as much to be trusted as the other boys. I don't expect he'll be silly again, do you?

# The Little
# Lost Brother

There were once two children called Alice
and Tommy. Alice was the older of the
two, for she was nine. Tommy was nearly
seven.

They lived with their mother and
father in a nice little house, and they
had a small, cosy room to play in, with
plenty of toys.

But dear me, Alice was so horrid to
Tommy! "You're a baby!" she said to him
a hundred times a day. "I don't know
why I should bother to play with you.
You don't even know your two times
table!"

"Teach me then," said good-tempered
little Tommy, who thought that Alice
was the cleverest, most wonderful girl
in the world. But Alice would never

bother to teach Tommy anything.

She was bigger than Tommy, and often pushed him and punched him. Tommy had been told that he musn't hit a girl, but it was sometimes very difficult not to slap Alice back when she was unkind to him.

Mother was often cross with Alice. "You quarrel all day long with poor Tommy," she said. "You interfere in his games. You call him names and smack him. You don't deserve a little brother to play with – and yet you were so pleased when he was born, to think you

would have someone to play with, instead of being alone all day."

"Tommy's silly," said Alice sulkily.

"No, he's not," said Mother. "When you were only six you didn't know even as much as Tommy does. You are growing into a very horrid little girl, and you don't deserve to have a nice little brother like Tommy."

The funny thing was that although Alice was always making fun of Tommy, and laughing at him, Tommy loved Alice with all his heart. He was a kindly little boy, and however much Alice had teased him, he would always go to her and kiss her goodnight when he went to bed. He thought Alice was wonderful.

One day Auntie Ellen came to lunch and tea. Alice was not good that day. She had a doll from her aunt and Tommy had an aeroplane – and Alice wanted the aeroplane instead of the doll. She tried to snatch it from Tommy's hand – and she broke one of the pretty silver wings.

"Oh!" said Tommy. "Look what you've done!"

"Well, you should have let me play with it," said Alice sulkily. "It was your fault."

"It certainly was not Tommy's fault," said Auntie Ellen at once. "It was yours. You really are unkind, Alice. You have broken Tommy's aeroplane. Now you must give him your doll."

"I shan't," said Alice. But Mother made her give up her doll, and although Tommy did not want to make Alice unhappy, he really did like to have a doll of his own for a change. It was a boy-doll too, so he called it Peter.

Alice waited till Auntie and Mother were out of the room, and then she rushed at Tommy. She grabbed the boy-doll and tried to pull it away. But Tommy held on.

The poor doll came in half! Its head came off and one of its legs. Tommy looked at it and howled.

"Stop making that noise," said Alice fiercely. "Mummy will come in."

"I'm not crying for myself, I'm crying for the p-p-p-poor hurt d-d-doll!" wept Tommy. "Its head has come off. It's dead".

"Be quiet," said Alice, and she slapped Tommy. And just then in came Auntie Ellen to see what was the matter. She looked angry when she saw the broken doll.

"What has happened?" she asked.

"Tommy wouldn't give me the doll, so we pulled it and it got broken," said Alice.

"I see," said Auntie. "And then, having broken his toy, you slapped him! Poor Tommy! It must be dreadful for him to have an unkind sister like you!"

"Well, I'm sure I don't want him for a brother," said Alice. "Silly baby thing! Wants to play with a doll, and he's a boy! I wish he'd go right away and leave me alone!"

The naughty little girl ran out of the room and slammed the door. Tommy sobbed. He couldn't bear to hear Alice speaking so unkindly of him. Auntie Ellen looked angrier than he had ever seen her. She went out to speak to Mother.

Alice ran out into the garden and hid under a bush. She was afraid Mother would call her and punish her. But Mother didn't. Alice heard a clock strike two and knew that she must get ready for school. So she crept indoors, washed her hands, took her hat and coat, and crept off to school without saying goodbye to anyone.

She wasn't very happy at school. But when it was over, she didn't feel very happy to go home either. She was afraid of what Auntie might say to her. She was always much firmer with her than her mother was. Oh dear! Bother silly Tommy and his doll!

At last Alice got home. She went into the sitting-room. Mother was there, sewing, but Tommy and Auntie were nowhere to be seen.

"Hello, Mummy," said Alice. "We did handicrafts at school this afternoon."

"Oh," said Mother. She looked sad. Alice loved her mother, although she was often rude and unkind to her, and she didn't like to see her looking unhappy. So she began to talk again.

"Mary Brown had 'very good' for her sums this morning," said Alice.

"Oh," said Mother, and went on sewing and looking sad.

"Where's Auntie?" asked Alice.

"She's gone home," said Mother.

"Oh," said Alice, feeling very glad. "And where's Tommy?"

"He's gone," said Mother.

"Gone!" said Alice. "Where's he gone?"

"He's gone home with Auntie," said Mother. "We thought that as you didn't want him for a brother, Auntie had better have him. She hasn't any children of her own, you know, and she and Uncle John love Tommy. So she took him home."

Alice stared as if she couldn't believe her ears. "But Tommy's ours," she said at last.

"Well, he's Auntie's now," said Mother. "You make him very unhappy, you know, Alice, although he loves you with all his heart. You were lucky to have such a kind, loving, generous little brother. Lots of boys are rough and rude, and haven't any time for their sisters. Tommy always loved to play with you, and thought you were wonderful."

"But, Mummy, won't you miss Tommy?" asked Alice, knowing now why her mother looked sad.

"Of course I shall," said Mother. "I feel very unhappy about it, especially now that Daddy has gone away to work. But I really can't have a nice little boy like Tommy living in a home where his sister wants to be alone. I want Tommy to be happy, and he does love Auntie Ellen and Uncle John. I can go round and see him every day."

Alice didn't know what to think. It was all very strange. She looked at her mother in dismay.

"Well, Alice," said Mother, "you should be very happy now. You have what you want – your little brother is out of your way and will not bother you any more."

Alice crept out of the room and went into the garden. She sat down on the seat and thought. She felt horrid. She hadn't really wanted Tommy to go away – and now he had.

"And Auntie Ellen loves him very much and she'll want to keep him always," said Alice to herself, "and I shan't have a brother at all!"

Just then Katie, next door, called over the fence:

"Hey, Alice! Where's Tommy? Larry wants to speak to him."

"He's gone away," said Alice. "Auntie's got him for her own."

Katie stared. "Really!" she said. "Oooh! How horrid for you! I'd hate our Larry to go away somewhere else. But you never liked your Tommy much, did you? So you'll be glad he's gone. I always thought you were so horrid to him, Alice, and he was such a dear little boy."

"Teatime!" called Mother, and Alice went in, still looking very glum. It was funny not seeing Tommy at teatime. His chair was empty.

Mother didn't want to talk, so it was a very quiet meal. Alice wished Tommy

was there to chatter and ask her all about her handicraft. He thought she was marvellous at it.

After tea there was no one to play with. Alice had a tent down in the garden, but it wasn't any fun playing by herself. You couldn't play catch or hide-and-seek by yourself. So she took her spade and dug a big castle in the sandpit.

"Tommy will like that," she said, when she had finished it. "I'll call him."

Then she remembered that it wasn't any good calling. Tommy wasn't there. Alice began to feel lonely. It wasn't nice without Tommy. He was a baby but still, he was fun to play with.

And perhaps he wasn't really a baby, either. He never cried when he fell down, as Larry did. And he could build clever things with Lego – better than Alice, really.

Bedtime was horrible too. It had been fun to watch Tommy being bathed, and sailing his duck and his ship in the water. Now there was nobody to watch. There was no little brother to kiss her goodnight and put his warm little arms round her neck, either.

Alice looked so sad when she was in bed that Mother was surprised.

"Well, really, Alice!" she said. "I should have thought you would have been very happy to have got your wish, and not have Tommy any more. Instead you look miserable."

Alice didn't say anything. She knew she would cry if she did. Mother didn't look at all happy either, and Alice knew that she was missing Tommy. She hated

Mother to look sad. She felt a very ashamed and unhappy little girl as she lay down to go to sleep that night.

She thought of Tommy's empty bed. She thought how Tommy had gone without sweets and saved up his pennies to buy her the doll's cot for her birthday that she had so badly wanted. She thought of his merry chuckles and the way his curly hair always fell over his face and had to be pushed back. She thought of how he always came and hugged her when she had hurt herself.

"Tommy is the nicest little brother in the world," wept poor Alice. "I do love him, though the others think I don't. I may have been horrid to him on top, but underneath I love him very much and I want him. I don't want Auntie to have him. He's mine. I've made Mummy unhappy too. I ought to be the one to go away, not Tommy."

She cried herself to sleep, and dreamed about Tommy all night. And in the morning, instead of going to school, what do you think she did? She ran off to her auntie's house, went down the garden, and found Tommy there, playing in the sandpit.

"Tommy!" cried Alice. "Tommy! Have you missed me? Oh, Tommy, do you like being here better than being with Mummy and me?"

Tommy looked at Alice. "No, I don't," he said. "But if you don't want me for a brother, Alice, I must go away. Auntie said so."

"But I do want you – I do!" said Alice, and the tears fell down her cheeks. "Don't remember the horrid things I've done, Tommy. I won't do them any more. I love you really, just like you love me, so please, please come back home with me. Oh, Tommy, do!"

"Of course I will, Alice!" said Tommy, and the little boy flung his arms round his sister and tried to wipe her tears away with his hand. "But don't let's tell Auntie. She might say I wasn't to go. She thought you were so horrid to me yesterday. But I don't mind, now you've come to get me back. You really do want

me to come home, don't you?"

"I really, really do," said Alice in such a very solemn voice that Tommy knew she was speaking the truth. So he ran home with her, without even getting his pyjamas, and Mother was so surprised to see him! She hugged him, and asked Alice what had happened.

"Mummy, I fetched him back," said Alice. "I want him. I'm sorry I was unkind and I'll never be again. Auntie's not to have him, because he's mine and yours. Will you tell Auntie that?"

"I'll tell her," said Mother, looking very happy. "Now you really must go to school, Alice. Hurry along."

How happy Alice was as she ran to school! Tommy would be waiting for her when she got back. She would give him the little blue-and-red train he had always loved of hers. She would jolly well show Auntie Ellen that Tommy was her brother and she loved him! Nobody should dare to take him away again!

So now Tommy is very happy. Alice is splendid to him, and teaches him

everything she can, and Mother is very happy too.

It's nice when brothers and sisters love one another, isn't it? I'm sure you wouldn't like to lose yours, like Alice nearly lost Tommy!

# James's
# Feather-Headdress

"Mum!" cried James, running indoors to where his mother was baking cakes. "Mum! Can I play cowboys and Indians this afternoon?"

"Yes, if you want to," said Mother.

"Well, I shall have to have a proper Indian headdress, then," said James. "You know, Mum, one with bright feathers all the way round. Harry and Bob have got them. I can't be an Indian without a proper headdress."

"Oh, James, I can't possibly buy you one today," said Mother. "For one thing I'm too busy, and for another they are rather expensive."

"Then I can't play cowboys and Indians," said James, rather sadly.

"I can't see why not," said Mother.

"Surely you can pretend, can't you?"

"Yes, I could pretend all right, but the others won't," said James. "You see, those who haven't got feather-headdresses are to be cowboys. And I do hate being a cowboy, Mum. I always have to be caught and tied to a tree."

"Well, darling, don't play with the others then," said Mother, and she popped a whole batch of cakes into the oven. "I want some books taken to Mr Oldfield this afternoon, and you can take those for me instead, if you like."

"Well, I don't really want to, Mum, but if I can't go and play I might as well do that," said James, gloomily. "I like Mr Oldfield's parrot. I'll take it some sunflower seeds out of my garden."

So that afternoon James set off to take the bundle of books to Mr Oldfield. He could hear the shouts of the other children as he went across the fields, and he wished and wished he was playing cowboys and Indians with them.

"But I won't be a cowboy any more," he thought. "It's no fun being a cowboy. The Indians always win."

He got to Mr Oldfield's and knocked at the door. The parrot cried, "Come in!" And James laughed and opened the door himself. The parrot was in a big cage, and her sharp eyes looked at James.

"Hello, Mr Oldfield," said James, shaking hands with the old man sitting reading in a chair. "Hello, Polly Parrot. How are you?"

"Got a pain in my tummy," said the parrot in such a comical voice that James laughed and laughed.

"Shut the door now, shut the door!" said the parrot. So James shut the door, and then gave Mr Oldfield the parcel of books.

"Thanks, James," said the old man. "It's nice of you to come all this way on this hot afternoon instead of playing games with the others."

"Well, you see, they're playing cowboys and Indians and I haven't any Indian feathers," explained James, "and I'm a bit tired of always being a cowboy."

"I should think so!" said Mr Oldfield.

"So should I!" said the parrot.

"Isn't your parrot clever?" said James. "She's the cleverest parrot I've ever known."

"Clever Polly, clever Polly," said the parrot, and laughed just like James did! She danced to and fro on her perch and then climbed all the way up her cage and down again.

"I've brought Polly some sunflower seeds from the giant sunflowers in my garden," said James. "Can I give them to her?"

"Certainly," said Mr Oldfield. "She will be delighted. It's very kind of you."

"Gobble, gobble, gobble!" said the parrot when she saw the seeds, and she snapped her beak together with joy.

"Polly looks rather dull and thin," said James, looking at the parrot.

"Yes, she has been moulting – changing her coat, you know," said Mr Oldfield. "She drops her feathers and grows nice new ones. She's doing it now. I've saved all the old feathers for you – look! You are so kind to her that I thought Polly would like you to have her colourful feathers."

Mr Oldfield took down a tall vase in which he had put all Polly's bright feathers as she had dropped them. They were green, blue, yellow, and red, as colourful as could be.

James was delighted. "Mr Oldfield!" he almost shouted. "They will do for Indian feathers! Oh, how wonderful! Just look at them – they will be marvellous! Oh, how I wish I knew how to sew them on to a band!"

"Dear me, now, what a very good idea," said Mr Oldfield, getting quite excited himself. "Well, I'll call my wife. She will be able to do a little sewing for us, I expect! Mary, Mary! Where are you?"

"Here, dear," said Mrs Oldfield, and she bustled in and smiled at James. "What's the matter?"

"Mary, could you possibly sew these parrot feathers on to a band of some sort so that James can wear them round his head like an Indian?" asked Mr Oldfield.

"Oh, easily!" said Mrs Oldfield. In no time she had taken out her thimble, scissors, needle and thread, and had found a broad piece of tape. She was soon sewing each bright feather neatly round the tape!

It was soon done, and she fitted it round James's head. Then she sewed it tightly, and let a piece hang down his back, covered with feathers.

He did look splendid! He looked at himself in the glass, and gave a cry of joy.

"I'm a real Indian! Oh, I do look grand! Thank you, Mrs Oldfield. Thank you, Polly Parrot."

"Don't mention it," said Polly, and gave a whoop like an Indian war-cry!

Off went James to join the other children – and they thought his feather-headdress was simply marvellous!

"The parrot gave the feathers to me," said James proudly. "And she showed me how to do a whoop – like this!"

And he gave such a terrible screech that everyone ran away in fright – the cowboys and the Indians too! I wish you had heard him!

# The Enchanted Toadstool

One day Daisy and Jack went for a picnic in Cuckoo Wood. They had their lunch in their pockets, and they wanted to find a nice cool place to eat in, for the day was very hot.

"Look at that little path," said Jack, pointing to a narrow winding way that left the main path and ran between the trees. "Shall we go down here, Daisy?"

"It's only a rabbit path, isn't it?" said Daisy. "We shan't get lost, shall we?"

"Oh, no!" said Jack. "This is only a small wood, you know. Come on."

So off they went down the winding rabbit path. They hadn't gone far before they saw a very curious sight.

"Did you see that?" asked Jack, in excitement. "That rabbit, Daisy! It had a pair of spectacles on its nose and it carried a bag under its arm."

"Yes!" said Daisy, with her eyes open very wide. "I did see it, Jack. Fancy that! Could we really have seen it, do you think?"

"We must have, if we both think we did," said Jack. "Oh, Daisy! Do let's go the way he went, and see if we can see him again!"

Off they ran, taking the same path as the rabbit. It wound between the trees, which got thicker and thicker.

"It must lead to the very middle of the wood," said Jack. "Isn't it dark here, Daisy? The sun can hardly get between the branches!"

"You're sure we shan't get lost, Jack?" said Daisy, nervously. "It would be awful if we couldn't find our way back."

"Look! there's the rabbit again!" said Jack.

Sure enough, there he was, hurrying along in front of them. The children ran faster.

Suddenly they came out into a round clear space, with oak-trees all around in a ring. In the very middle was a large toadstool with red spots. The rabbit sat on this, called out something in a loud voice, and then, hey presto, the toadstool sank swiftly down into the earth and disappeared, taking the rabbit with it!

"Good gracious!" said Daisy, startled. "Just look at that, Jack! Where has he gone?"

"Into the earth!" said Jack, astonished. "Come and see!"

They ran to the place where the rabbit

and the toadstool had disappeared, and looked at it carefully. There was no sign of anything at all. The grass grew there exactly as it grew all round.

Then suddenly the toadstool came back! It shot up out of the earth just as if it was growing very fast, and caught Jack under the chin. Over he went and over and over, for the toadstool gave him quite a blow. Daisy ran to him and asked him if he was hurt.

"No," said Jack, rubbing his chin. "Only surprised, that's all! Fancy it coming back like that, Daisy! And without the rabbit too! Where has he gone, I wonder?"

"I don't know," said Daisy. "Isn't it

funny, Jack! It's like a story in a book."

The children went to the toadstool again and looked at it.

"Did you hear what the rabbit said when he sat on it?" asked Daisy.

"It sounded something like 'Hi-tiddley-hi-toe, down we go to the land below'." said Jack.

"Let's sit on it for a moment!" said Daisy. "It would be so exciting! But don't you say what the rabbit said, because I don't want to go down into the earth like that!"

Jack sat on the toadstool. He was just making room for Daisy, when a loud voice cried out:

"Hi-tiddley-hi-toe, down you go to the land below!"

And then, oh dear me! The toadstool shot downwards, taking Jack with it! Daisy was left standing alone, her eyes and mouth wide open with fright.

"He's gone!" said the voice again, and Daisy looked round to see a grinning gnome, who thought he had played a fine trick on Jack.

"What did you do that for?" said Daisy, too angry to wonder at the sight of a gnome. "Make the toadstool come back again with Jack on it."

"Can't be done!" said the gnome, with a chuckle. "Why don't you sit on it and go down too?"

"I'm afraid," said Daisy. "Oh, you horrid little gnome, you'd no right to send the toadstool down like that!"

"Why not?" asked the gnome. "It's my toadstool! Your brother shouldn't have sat on it without asking my permission!"

"Well, we saw a rabbit sitting on it," said Daisy.

"He's my servant," said the gnome. "He's gone to take a message for me to my cousin the Blue Goblin. He's allowed to use my toadstool whenever he likes."

"Will the Blue Goblin send Jack back safely?" asked Daisy.

"I don't know," said the gnome.

"Then as soon as the toadstool comes back I shall go and find out!" said Daisy. As she spoke the toadstool suddenly reappeared, and she ran to it. She sat down on it and called out, "Hi-tiddley-hi-toe, down we go to the land below!"

In a flash she felt the toadstool sinking

swiftly into the ground, and she clutched at the sides. Down it went and down and down. Then *bump*! It came to a standstill and Daisy was shot off.

She stood up and found herself in a round room, very small and lit only by a glow-worm in a glass lamp. The toadstool suddenly shot upwards again, and made Daisy jump. She looked all round for her brother, but she could see him nowhere in the little room. There was no one, and nothing there except the tiny lamp.

"Where's the door?" thought Daisy. She felt all round the room, and at first could find no way of getting out at all. Then she suddenly came to a tiny knob about three feet up the wall. She pressed it, and an opening came, just big enough for her to slip through.

On the other side was a passage, lit by more glow-worm lamps. She made her way down it, and at last came to three turnstiles, each standing at the entrance to three passages. She stood outside them, and wondered which Jack had gone through.

She could see no one to ask for advice, so she pushed through the middle turnstile and ran on down the passage. It led to a yellow door, and she knocked on it.

"Come in, come in, come in!" called a voice. Daisy opened the door and went through. She found herself in a cellar, and saw a flight of stone steps leading up to an open trapdoor. She went up them, and saw a small room in which a brownie sat. He had a very long beard and a long nose. He was writing quickly in a big book, with a large quill pen.

He looked up as Daisy stepped into the room, but didn't seem at all surprised to see her.

"Please, could you tell me where my brother Jack is?" asked Daisy.

"He hasn't been through here," said the brownie, dipping his pen carefully in the ink. "He probably went through one of the other turnstiles."

"Oh dear!" said Daisy in dismay. "Have I got to go right back through that dark passage again?"

134

"Not unless you want to," said the brownie. "I can find out where your brother is in no time, if you will pay me one penny."

"Here's a penny Daddy gave me last Saturday," said Daisy, and she gave him a nice bright penny. He put it in his pocket, and then picked up a large mirror.

"Come here," he said to Daisy. "Look into this mirror and think of your brother."

Daisy looked into the mirror, and to her great surprise she could not see herself at all. She thought of Jack, and there came a picture into the mirror of a little boy sitting on a chair, peeling potatoes, while a rabbit with spectacles on his nose was watching him.

"Oh, there's Jack, and there's that rabbit we saw!" cried Daisy. "But I don't know now where Jack really is, Mr Brownie. Do you?"

The brownie put on a pair of blue spectacles and peered into the magic mirror.

"Yes," he said at last. "He's in the kitchen of the Blue Goblin, and I'm afraid he's a prisoner. That rabbit led him there."

Daisy began to cry, and this upset the brownie very much.

"Don't do that," he begged. "I can't bear it. I'll help you all I can."

"How can I save Jack from being a prisoner?" asked Daisy, still crying.

"I don't know," said the brownie, pulling at his long beard. "I never heard of anyone escaping from the Blue Goblin."

"Can't anyone save him?" asked Daisy.

"Well, there's the Dumpy Wizard, who's very kind and very clever," said the brownie. "He might be able to tell you how to rescue Jack. He lives on Blowaway Hill, a good way from here. You could go and ask him."

"Thank you very much," said Daisy, drying her eyes. "Which way shall I go?"

The brownie took her to his door, and pointed out a steep hill in the distance.

"Do you see that castle?" he asked. "Well, that's where the Dumpy Wizard lives. But it's very, very difficult to see him, so people say."

Daisy thanked the brownie and started off in the direction of the castle. She went along a lane whose hedges were starred with the loveliest flowers she had ever seen. She met fairy folk of all kinds, and they seemed just as surprised to see her as she was to see them. She asked her way several times, and at last she seemed to be getting nearer to the hill.

Soon she came to a stile and climbed over it. On the other side was a small elf, crying bitterly, and Daisy stopped to ask what was the matter.

"Look!" said the elf. "I've broken my lovely new necklace! All the beads have rolled here, there and everywhere! I can't find them because I have left my glasses at home, and I can't see very well without them."

"I'll find them for you," said Daisy. She went down on her hands and knees and looked for the beads. They were very

138

small, but Daisy had sharp eyes, and soon she had quite a lot to give the little elf. He counted them, and thanked her very much.

"There are only three missing now," he said. "It is so kind of you to have helped me. I've got three extra beads at home, so don't bother to look any more. Where are you going?"

"To Wizard Dumpy's castle," said Daisy. "I'm going to ask his help for something."

"Then you may find this useful," said the elf, and pushed something into Daisy's hand. She looked at it and found that it was a tiny key. She was just going

to ask the elf what it was for when she saw that he had vanished. She went on her way towards the hill, wondering how she could find such a tiny little key at all useful.

At last she came to the hill. It was very, very steep indeed. A narrow little path led up to it and Daisy started to climb it. Soon she noticed a pixie in front of her, carrying a heavy basket. She caught her up and asked if she could help her.

"I'm very strong," said Daisy. "Do let me help you. I could take one side of the basket."

"Thank you," said the pixie, surprised and pleased. "Where are you going?"

"To the castle," said Daisy. "I want to ask the wizard's help."

"He's very difficult to see," said the pixie, giving Daisy one side of the basket to carry. "People say that he is quite impossible to get at, so there isn't much hope for you."

Daisy sighed. It would be dreadful to come all this way and not be able to get help at the end.

"Are you going to the castle?" she asked the pixie.

"No," said she. "I'm going to my cottage just near by. Won't you come in and have a cup of tea with me?"

"I mustn't, thank you," said Daisy. "I really must see the wizard as soon as I can."

Just then they arrived at the pixie's cottage. She took the basket from Daisy, and thanked her very much for her kind help.

"Here's something to take with you,"

she said, running into her house. "You may find it useful."

Daisy wondered whether she was going to be given another key but to her surprise the pixie gave her a little stool!

Daisy tucked it under her arm and said thank you, though she would really much rather not have had it to carry. Off she went again up the hill. The castle seemed very near now.

As Daisy climbed up the steep path, she suddenly felt very hungry. She remembered that she had a packet of sandwiches in her pocket and she stopped to get them out. She found them and took the paper off. How good the sandwiches smelled!

She sat down to eat them. Just as she was beginning, an old woman, rather like a witch, came down the hill. When she saw Daisy she stopped.

"Spare me a little of your lunch!" she begged. "I am so hungry. I haven't a penny in the world, and if you don't let me share your meal, I shall get nothing all day long."

Daisy looked at her. She certainly seemed thin and poor. Her shawl was torn and her shoes were in holes. She carried a very long stick with a crook at the end, much taller than herself.

"Here you are," said Daisy, dividing her sandwiches in half. "Here are three for you, old woman. And wait a minute! I believe I've got a bar of chocolate here. You can have half of that too."

The old woman sat down by Daisy, and ate hungrily.

"Where are you going?" she asked.

"To see the wizard in the castle," said Daisy.

"But you'll never do that!" said the old woman. "He won't see anyone, you know!"

"Oh dear!" said Daisy, nearly crying. "Everyone tells me that. I do so hope he will see me!"

The old woman said nothing more until she had finished her sandwiches. Then she rose to her feet, and spoke to Daisy again.

"Thank you very much for your kindness," she said. "I haven't anything much to give you in return, but please take this stick. You may find it useful."

Daisy took the very long stick, wondering how she could ever find such a thing useful. She thanked the old woman and once more went up the hill. Soon she came to the castle gate, and as it was open she went through it.

There were about a hundred steps leading up to the castle door, and Daisy climbed them all, being very much out of

breath when she came to the top. She knocked on the door with the great knocker there, and a small gnome opened it.

"Please can I see the wizard?" asked Daisy politely.

"You can't," said the gnome. "He's shut up in his tower and no one can get to him."

"Oh, please do let me see him!" said Daisy.

"But I tell you, you can't," said the gnome. "Not even his servants can get to see him today. He's writing a lot of learned spells, and can't be interrupted unless it's for anything tremendously important."

"Well, what I've got to ask him *is* tremendously important," said Daisy. "Please, please, do tell him."

"Now look here," said the gnome, impatiently, "I tell you I can't tell him. Come in and I'll show you why."

Daisy followed the gnome into the hall, and into a large room on the right hand side. At the end was a small door with a pane of glass let into it.

"Look through that pane," said the gnome. "Do you see a loop of rope up in the far corner?"

"Yes," said Daisy.

"Well," said the gnome. "When that rope is pulled it rings a bell very loudly in the wizard's tower. Then he leaves his work and comes to see his visitor."

"Well, why can't you pull the rope?" asked Daisy.

"For lots of reasons," said the gnome.
"For one thing the door is locked! For
another thing I can't reach the rope!
Now don't be impatient, little girl. Just
sit down quietly in this chair and wait
until the wizard finishes his work. He
may take all day or he may take a week,
I can't tell you."

Daisy was in despair. She sat down on
the chair and thought of poor Jack. She
looked round to tell the gnome that she

couldn't stay, she would have to go and see the Blue Goblin, when she saw that he had gone. She was alone.

She waited for a little while, and then she felt the tears trickling down her face. She put her hand in her pocket to get out her handkerchief and there she felt the little key that the elf had given her.

She took it out and looked at it. It was very tiny. Suddenly an idea came to her. She jumped up and ran to the little door through which she had seen the rope. She fitted the key into the lock and turned it.

It was the very key for the door! It swung open and, quickly picking up her stool and long stick, Daisy went through, carefully shutting the door behind her in case the little gnome came back and was angry with her.

She looked up at the rope in the corner. It was far too high for her to reach. She suddenly wondered if the long stick that the old woman had given her would reach it. She tried – but alas, it was a little too short. Try as she would Daisy couldn't get the crook handle of the stick into the loop of the rope. Then suddenly she gave a cry of joy.

"My stool!" she shouted. "If I stand on the stool that the pixie gave me, I may be able to reach it!"

She put it under the rope, and stood on it. Then she reached up with her stick – and, hey presto, she could just slip the crook handle into the loop! She did so, and pulled hard at the rope.

There came a tremendous noise of ringing bells, so loud that Daisy was almost deafened. Then came the sound of running footsteps and the little gnome burst angrily into the room.

"How dare you, how dare you!" he cried. "My master will turn you into an earwig for disturbing him!"

"Silence!" a deep voice cried suddenly, and Daisy and the gnome turned to the door. The Dumpy Wizard himself stood there. He was round and fat, not much bigger than Daisy herself, but very, very wise-looking.

"Who rang that bell?" he asked.

"I did," said Daisy, bravely. "I wanted to ask your help."

"How did you get the key to open this door?" asked the wizard, "and the long stick?"

Daisy told him, and when she had finished he smiled very kindly.

"Ah, I can see you have been doing some kind deeds," he said, "so I cannot refuse to help you. What do you want me to do?"

"Please, could you rescue my brother Jack?" begged Daisy. "The Blue Goblin has got him as a servant."

"Certainly," said the wizard. Then he turned to his astonished servant. "Fetch my carriage," he ordered.

In a minute or two a grand carriage, pulled by seven white horses, was at the door. The Dumpy Wizard and Daisy stepped into it, and they drove off. After about half an hour they drew up at another castle, and the wizard thumped loudly at the door.

A goblin, who was dressed all in blue, answered it.

"Where's that boy you've got?" demanded the wizard.

"You must be mistaken, your highness!" said the goblin, trembling. "I have no boy!"

"WHERE'S THAT BOY YOU'VE GOT?" said the wizard in a very frightening voice.

The goblin said no more. He disappeared into his castle, and came back again with – who do you think? – Yes, Jack! How glad Daisy was! She leaped out of the carriage and ran to meet him. They hugged one another and cried for joy.

The Blue Goblin vanished into his castle and banged the door. The Dumpy Wizard put both his arms round the two children and laughed and cried with them, he was so pleased to see two people so happy.

"You should be proud of your sister," he said to Jack. "She has been very brave. Now would you like me to drive you home?"

"Oh, please do!" said Daisy. So they all climbed into the carriage again, and off went the seven horses at a spanking rate. And in ten minutes they were driving down the village street where Daisy and Jack lived! What a stir there was in the little place! Everyone turned out to see them!

They said goodbye to the Dumpy Wizard and he drove off again. Then they ran indoors to tell their mother all their wonderful adventures. She was just as excited as they were.

"Tomorrow you shall take me into the woods to see that enchanted toadstool!" she said. "And I'll just tell that gnome what a wicked creature he is for letting his rabbit take Jack to the Blue Goblin."

But do you know, when they got to the little round clearing, there was no toadstool there at all! They couldn't see the gnome either, so they thought he must have gone away in case someone should come and scold him for what he had done. All they saw was a solemn grey rabbit peering at them from behind a bush.

"Is that the rabbit who took you away, Jack?" cried Daisy – but before they could see for certain, he was gone! Still, I shouldn't be surprised if he was the rabbit, would you?

# The Top that Ran Away

Once there was a humming top who was very proud indeed of his humming and spinning. He spun himself round all day long till the other toys got quite giddy with watching him. He hummed all the time, too. "Zoooooooooooom!" he sang. "Zoooooooooooom!"

"Do stop," said the baby doll. "I'm tired of hearing you."

"Yes, lie down and have a rest," said the wooden soldier. "You make me tired."

"You are jealous of me because I can spin and hum and none of you can do the same!" sang the top, zooming even more loudly. "I shall run away from you. You are selfish, stupid toys! I shall go out into the big world and hum and spin all I like."

"Go then," said the wooden soldier. "You'll be sorry. It isn't often that toys have a beautiful playroom like this to live in and a kind little girl like Katie to play with them." The top spun round quickly.

"Zooooooooooom!" it said. "There are better things than this! Goodbye!"

It spun itself out of the playroom and down the stairs, out of the back door and down the garden path – and into the road! "Zooooooooooom!" it went.

It met a duck waddling along. The duck stared in surprise.

"Zooooooooooom!" said the top. "I'm a wonder, I am! See me spin! Hear me hum! Zooooooooooom! Can you do that, Duck?"

"Quack!" said the duck. "No, I've never seen anyone like you before. I don't like you." The duck pecked at the top and it almost lost its balance and fell. It zoomed angrily and spun away down the lane. Soon it met a kitten chasing a piece of paper.

"Zooooooooooom!" said the top. "I'm a wonder, I am! See me spin! Hear me

hum! Zoooom! Can you do that?"

"Miaow!" said the kitten in alarm. "No, I can't go round like that – it's silly. And why should I hum if I can mew? Get off my piece of paper. I'm playing with it."

The top spun round on the paper and wouldn't get off. The kitten crouched and sprang. Her claws scratched the shining top and made marks on it. The top spun crookedly and zoomed crossly. It spun away from the kitten and went on its way.

Then it met a big cow and spun between its feet.

"Zoooooooooooom!" said the top. "I'm a wonder I am! See me spin! Hear me hum! Zoooom! Can you do that?"

"Moo!" said the cow in surprise. "Of course not. What do you suppose the farmer would say if I began to spin round on one leg and make a noise like a young aeroplane? Get away from my feet. You'll trip me up."

The top wouldn't get away. It went proudly spinning and zooming. The cow kicked it. What a shock for the top! It

almost stopped spinning and very nearly fell over. But it saved itself and then went on down the lane, still zooming at the top of its voice.

The next creature it met was a worm, and the top spun right up to it.

"Zoooom!" said the top. "I'm a wonder, I am! See me spin! Hear me hum! Zooooom! Can you do that?"

"No," said the worm in fright, "and I don't want to either. If I spun round like that, all the birds of the air would see me and come flying down to get me. And no worm would make a terrible noise like that! Oooooh! Don't spin on me, Top, you're hurting me!"

The top was most unkindly spinning on the worm's tail. The worm wriggled free and shot down its hole at top speed. The top was pleased.

My, what a grand time it was having, spinning and frightening everyone out in the big world!

Soon the top came to where a large spider was talking to a bumble-bee. "Zooooooom!" said the top. "I'm a wonder, I am. See me spin! Hear me hum! Zooooom! Can you do that?"

"I can hum," said the bumble-bee quietly.

"And I can spin," said the spider, looking at the top with her eight eyes. "Don't spoil my web, Top."

But the top did spoil it. It spun and it broke it. The spider said nothing. "You are not telling the truth," said the top rudely. "You cannot spin! No one but a humming top can spin! I'm a wonder, I am."

"Stay here for the night and I will show you how I and my family can spin," said the spider. "Bumble-bee, go and fetch all my family – the biggest you can find."

The bumble-bee flew off, zooming through the air just like a big humming-top. Soon he was back and hurrying over the ground below him came twenty big garden-spiders.

"Now we will show you how we spin," said the spider. "Bumble-bee, sing us a tune – for very soon the top will cease to hum! Sisters, begin your work! Spin well!"

The top hummed angrily and more loudly than ever as it spun round and round among the long-legged spiders. Quietly they began to spin out their silken threads. The wind took the threads into the air and wound them round the spinning top. More and more threads floated out from the spiders' bodies. More and more quickly they spun them. Soon hundreds of strong silky threads were fastened round the top.

It began to find it difficult to spin so fast. The threads pulled against it. The top spun more slowly and more slowly and yet more slowly! Its voice became fainter. The bee's loud hum could be heard above its own faint zoom.

"What are you doing – what are you doing?" hummed the top faintly.

"We are spinning, spinning, spinning," said the spider. "Not quite your kind of spinning, perhaps – but spinning all the same. We are spinning threads that will stop your spinning, proud and haughty top! Ah! Others can spin and hum too, you see!"

The top wobbled and wobbled – and stopped. It fell over on its side. It could not spin any longer, for the spiders' threads held it too tightly. The bumble-bee hummed in joy.

The spiders laughed among themselves and hurried away to spin big webs to catch flies for their dinner. The bumble-bee flew off to his hole in the bank. The top was left on the ground alone.

It began to rain. The pelting raindrops washed some of the bright paint off the top. It groaned to itself. "I shall get rusty now! Oh, why did I leave the playroom? Why was I so vain? I wish I was back!"

Well, the top got its wish – for not long after that, who should come by but Katie herself, going home after school. She saw her top lying in the rain, and she picked it up in surprise. The rain had washed the webs away. Katie didn't know that the top had been fastened down by them. She could not understand how the top had got there.

"Who took you out here, poor old top?" she said. "The rain will spoil you. I will take you in."

So the top got back to its own playroom and the toys stared in astonishment. The top lay down in the cupboard quite quietly. It didn't spin. It didn't hum.

"What's the matter with you?" asked the baby doll.

"Oh, I met other people in the big world who could spin and hum better than I could," said the top. "That's all."

The toys never knew who the top had met. I expect you wonder how I knew. Well, perhaps I heard the bumble-bee telling the foxgloves in my garden.

# He Wouldn't
# Buy a Ticket

Mr Scrimp was very mean with his money. When he went to market he always haggled with Dame Plump over her lovely butter, and beat her down a penny or two. And he would never pay Mother Silver-Top what she asked for her eggs.

"He's a mean old thing," said everyone in Apple-Tree Village. "He never even gives a penny to a child, or remembers anyone's birthday. Nasty old Scrimp."

Scrimp spent his money on himself. He liked beautiful things, which was rather strange because he had an ugly nature and a cold heart.

"I'll buy that lovely picture," he would say, and he would give quite a lot of money for the picture he wanted.

"I'll buy that carpet!"

"I'll buy that mirror! It's so beautiful."

"I'll buy that tea-set with the apple blossom all round it. It's lovely."

They were the sort of things he said, and his cottage was soon full of really lovely treasures. How he polished and cleaned them! He was proud of them, but when he asked people in to see them he never even offered them a cup of tea!

"Fancy that now!" said kind Dame Plump. "I went in to see that new vase he has bought and a beautiful thing it is too, and I took him a pat of my best butter and although the kettle was boiling on the hob and he'd got a whole plate of sugar biscuits set out for his tea, he never so much as offered me a crumb!"

"Disgusting," said everyone. "Well, well – he'll be sorry some day. That's not the way to get friends round you. He soon won't have a friend in Apple-Tree Village!"

Mr Scrimp didn't mind that. Friends meant that he would have to give them tea or a cup of cocoa or offer them a bun. He didn't like that. Let everyone keep away! Then he would have more money to spend on lovely things for himself.

Now, Mr Scrimp had an old mother who lived some miles away, in Cherry-Tree Village. She was about the only person he was fond of, and he went to see her once a week. But he didn't take her any presents – oh no! What, pick some flowers from his garden, or buy the peppermint sweets she loved! Of course not!

"You buy a pat of my butter to take to that poor old mother of yours," Dame Plump said to him once. But Mr Scrimp didn't even answer. Spend his money on butter for his mother! What next!

One day, when he was polishing a new and very beautiful tray he had bought for himself, a man drew up outside in a cart. He was on his way to the market. He called to Mr Scrimp.

"Hey, Mr Scrimp. I've got a message for you from Cherry-Tree Village. I've just come from there. Your poor old mother is very ill. Oh, very ill indeed, and she's calling out for you all day long. You'd better pack and go."

"Oh dear, oh dear!" said Mr Scrimp, in dismay. "My poor old mother! She seemed all right last week. Is she in bed?"

"Of course," said the man, clicking to his horse. "She had a bad fall two days ago. You'd better get along there quickly if you want to see the poor old lady alive."

Mr Scrimp was very upset. He ran in to his next-door neighbour, Mrs Helpful. "Oh, what shall I do? My old mother is very ill. I must go to her. But what about my hens?"

"Now, now, don't you worry a bit," said Mrs Helpful, sorry to see Mr Scrimp's pale face. "I'll see to your hens for you. You pack your bag and go. I'll pop in each day and dust round to keep all your treasures nice for you. You go straight away now, Mr Scrimp – and take a bunch of flowers from my garden for the old

lady, and this packet of sweets. Maybe she'll be better when she sees you."

Mr Scrimp picked a bunch of flowers from Mrs Helpful's garden, but he didn't pick any from his own. His mother would think they were from him. He would just tell her that Mrs Helpful had sent the sweets, but not say anything about the flowers.

He packed his bag quickly. Before he had finished many of the villagers came to tell him they were sorry to hear about his old mother.

"Mothers are very precious," said Dame Plump. "You take care of yours. She's been a good mother to you. Give her this bit of butter with my love."

"And don't you worry about all your beautiful things!" said Mrs Helpful. "We'll look after them for you. Now cheer up, Mr Scrimp, and give your mother our best wishes."

Mr Scrimp caught the next bus to Cherry-Tree Village. He found his old mother very ill indeed. She was so pleased to see him, and took his hand in hers.

"I'm glad to see you, son," she said.

"You will stay with me, won't you? Oh, what lovely flowers – and these sweets, too – and the butter! Why, you must love me after all! You've never brought me anything before, you know, son, and I've worried because I thought your heart was like a stone. Nobody can be happy with a cold heart. But yours must be warm after all, because look at the things you've brought me!"

Mr Scrimp didn't like to say that they were not from him, so he just held his mother's hand and nodded. "Now just you lie and rest, Mother," he said. "I'll stay with you till you're better."

His old mother looked at him happily. Why, her son couldn't be the mean, cold-hearted person that nobody seemed to like. Hadn't he left his nice cottage and all its beautiful things to come to her? Hadn't he brought her presents?

When her friends came in to see her, the old lady talked about her son. "He's so kind," she said. "So generous. Left his nice cottage and all his treasures to come and be with me. Brought me so many presents, too – do you see those lovely flowers? They must have been the best in his garden."

The carter who had brought the message to Mr Scrimp came to see her too. The old lady told him the same thing. He went back to Apple-Tree Village and repeated it to everyone.

"Well, would you think mean old Mr Scrimp was so nice after all?" said Dame Plump. "It just shows how you can make a mistake about people."

Mr Scrimp didn't buy his mother any more flowers. He didn't give a penny to any of the children who brought little gifts from their mothers. He wouldn't give anything towards a present for the village nurse, who came every day to see to his old mother.

And when someone came collecting at the door for a fund to buy things for somebody in Apple-Tree Village, his own town, he slammed the door in the surprised woman's face.

"What nonsense!" he said to his mother, when he told her about it.

"Collecting for somebody in my village! They've all got plenty of money. I won't give a penny!"

"Didn't you even find out who it was for?" said the old lady. "It might be for someone who is in real need of it, son."

"There's nobody who's in need of it!" said Mr Scrimp. "And I ought to know, oughtn't I?"

And then somebody came round selling tickets. "It's for a fair that is being held at Apple-Tree Village," explained the little woman with the tickets. "You see, they are doing their best to get a large sum to give to this person who has lost—"

"Well I never! Collecting for that person again! Who is he, I'd like to know! I'm from Apple-Tree Village myself, and I tell you this, I wouldn't buy a ticket to help anyone there. So don't come here again!"

Now, when his mother was better, Mr Scrimp packed his bag again, said goodbye and went. He caught the bus to Apple-Tree Village. The fair was on, and flags were up. There was even a roundabout.

"Come and buy a ticket!" called a child. "Come and have some fun!"

"Buy a ticket!" snorted Mr Scrimp. "What nonsense. Hey, Dame Plump, a word with you, please. What's all this about getting a fund for somebody in the village? They even came bothering me at Cherry-Tree Village to buy tickets! Such nonsense!"

Dame Plump looked at Mr Scrimp, and for a little while she didn't say anything.

"Well, Mr Scrimp," she said at last, "I will tell you about this man. You know him quite well. He went away, feeling

troubled and anxious over something, and we were sorry for him. And while he was away thieves broke in and stole almost everything from his cottage. They just left the kitchen stove and a broken chair and old sofa. Nothing else."

"Well, he's still got something left," said Mr Scrimp, impatiently. "Quite enough!"

"Perhaps you are right," said Dame Plump. "Well, Mrs Helpful was very upset and started this fund, and we thought we'd run a fair too, and all the money we made we would put towards buying furniture for the cottage – so that when this poor man came back he would at least find a bed, a table and things like that."

"What nonsense!" said Mr Scrimp. "Let him work a bit and earn money to buy them himself. Silly, soft-hearted lot you are. I wouldn't buy a ticket to help. I'm a sensible man. Where does this fellow live?"

"In your street," said Dame Plump. "Well, Mr Scrimp, I'm glad to have your advice. You really think we are foolish to be generous and kind over the matter? What do you think we ought to do with the money we've collected?"

"Oh, use it yourselves!" said Mr Scrimp impatiently. "Buy anything you want. But don't ask me for help!"

He stalked off down the street. Dame Plump followed him a little way behind. He came to his cottage, and put his key in the front door. He opened it – and then he stared in the utmost dismay!

The hall was empty. The hall-chair was gone, the mat was gone, the umbrella-stand wasn't there! The stair-carpet was gone. Mr Scrimp went into his sitting-room and looked round in horrified surprise.

There was only a broken chair and an old sofa in it. Nothing else at all. Gone were his beautiful mirror, his lovely vase, his bright carpet, his pretty tea-set.

In horror Mr Scrimp went into the other rooms. They were empty. The thieves had done a thorough job and had taken everything worth taking – and there had been a lot of valuable things in Mr Scrimp's cottage for robbers to take!

"I've been robbed! I've got nothing left!" groaned Mr Scrimp, sitting down heavily on the old sofa. "I've no money either, for I spent it all on my treasures. I'm a poor, miserable fellow who has been robbed of everything he possesses!"

Dame Plump came in with Mrs Helpful. They both looked rather stern.

"Mr Scrimp, we are sorry you have had to come back to such a desolate, empty cottage," said Mrs Helpful. "You can see what has happened. We were so sorry about it that we started a fund for you, and wanted to run a fair so that we could buy new things for you with the money."

"But now that we know you think such an idea is all nonsense, we will certainly do as you say, and spend the money on ourselves," said Dame Plump. "What a mean creature you are, Mr Scrimp! You wouldn't even buy a ticket to help someone in need – and now you discover that it was yourself we wanted to help, I expect you'd like to change your mind!"

The two women went out. Mr Scrimp groaned. If only he hadn't been so mean! The people of Apple-Tree Village must have got such a lot of money for him. They could have bought him all his furniture. Now he only had the sofa, the chair and the kitchen stove.

Mrs Helpful came in that evening after the fair. Mr Scrimp had dug up some potatoes from his garden and was trying to boil them on the stove in an old tin.

"Mr Scrimp," said Mrs Helpful, "we collected over a hundred pounds. But we are going to spend it on the children of this village, and lay out a playground for them with swings and sand-pits. I'm sorry we couldn't spend it on you, but we don't feel that someone as mean as you should have any money."

"You're right," said Mr Scrimp. "I'm ashamed of myself. I should have been warm-hearted and generous when I heard of someone whose goods had been stolen – I can tell you, Mrs Helpful, I know what it's like now to feel poor and unhappy – I'd give anything to have a little kindness shown me, but I shan't get any. And it serves me right!"

Mrs Helpful looked at him, trying to cook his potatoes in a tin. "You come along and have supper with me," she said. "Mr Helpful will lend you a few things, I'm sure – another chair – an old bed – a bit of mat for your feet. You come along."

"Well, I was never so glad of a bit of kindness in my life!" said Mr Scrimp.

"Do you mean it? Mrs Helpful, you warm my cold heart!"

"Do I?" said Mrs Helpful. "Now you listen to me, Mr Scrimp. See that your heart keeps warm, and do a bit of kindness to others. Loving-kindness is the biggest thing in the world. You try it!"

So Mr Scrimp is trying it, and he says Mrs Helpful is quite right – it is the biggest and best thing in the world!

# The
# Runaway Cows

Tom, Dick, Harry and Will were coming home from school one day, when they saw five red and white cows walking down the road.

"Look at those cows!" said Tom. "All by themselves! They must have got out of the field and run away!"

"They belong to Farmer White," said Dick. "Won't he be wild?"

"We'd better tell him," said Harry.

"No, we won't," said Will. "He's a horrid man. He shouts at boys and girls. And you know he won't let anyone go blackberrying in that field where the hedges are simply covered with big blackberries."

"So we won't bother about his old cows," said Tom. "We'll let them run

185

right away, and perhaps be knocked down by cars."

"That's not right," said Dick at once. "Why should we let the cows come to harm just because we don't like the farmer? You're always saying things like that, Tom."

"Well, anyway, why should we bother?" said Will, lazily. "It's not our business. They're not our cows. Nobody can make us go and tell the farmer they are loose."

"That's just it," said Harry. "Nobody *can* make us – it isn't our business – but if somebody doesn't take some trouble about those cows, they'll be hurt. We ought to make it our job to see they aren't."

"Well, all I say is, I hope that horrid farmer's cows do get hurt," said Tom, who was spiteful. "I'm going home."

"And I jolly well won't bother myself to go out of my way to tell the farmer," said Will. "I want my tea." So he went home with Tom.

Dick and Harry looked at one another. They were both sensible boys who liked

186

animals and would not let them get hurt if they could help it.

"It's true we don't like Farmer White," said Harry, "but all the same we ought to go and tell him. I'll go, Dick, and you chase after the cows and try and head them back." So Dick chased after the cows and managed to turn them back up the road again, while Harry went to tell the farmer.

He was having his tea. "What's up?" he said, when he saw Harry.

"Five of your cows are loose on the road, sir," said Harry. "Dick's gone to turn them back, but perhaps you had better come and take them to their field. Dick isn't very used to cows."

"Thanks," said the farmer, getting up. "It's nice to see a boy who'll take the trouble to put things right without being asked to! I'll come right now."

They went out and soon met Dick with the cows. He had found a stick and was feeling quite important chasing the cows back to the farm.

"Good of you to trouble," said the farmer. "I must find out who left my gate open. Just go ahead and see if it's shut or open now, will you?"

It was open. "There you are!" said the farmer crossly. "Some silly boy left it open, I suppose, in spite of the notice on it, Please Shut This Gate. Well – I should think all boys were silly and tiresome if you hadn't given me your help today. Thank you."

"Very pleased to help you," said Dick politely. Just as they were going, the

farmer turned back and shouted:

"Hey! Do you like blackberries?"

"Oh yes!" said both the boys.

"Well, there are some fine ones on the hedge in that field over there," said the farmer, pointing with his finger. "You and your friend can go and pick them whenever you like. I won't let other boys into the field because they leave the gate open."

"Oh, thanks!" said Dick and Harry in delight. Goodness – they would be able to take big baskets home full of ripe blackberries tomorrow.

"What a bit of luck!" said Harry, as they went home. "Weren't Tom and Will silly not to come and help with the cows too?"

The next day the two boys went to get the blackberries. They filled two big baskets and took them home.

On the way back they met Tom and Will. How the boys stared when they saw the enormous blackberries.

"We got them in the field over there," said Dick, pointing.

"You're not allowed to go there," said Will at once.

"Yes, we are. The farmer said we could," said Dick, and told Will and Tom all that had happened the day before.

"Take us with you tomorrow," said Tom. Harry shook his head.

"No," he said. "You wouldn't help yesterday, Tom, and we did. We didn't expect a reward, of course, but it was nice to get one. If you'd helped, you would have shared. As it is, the farmer said that only Dick and I were to go."

"Well, I shall help next time!" said Tom, looking ashamed. "I'm glad the cows weren't hurt. You deserve the blackberries, Harry!"

How they enjoyed the blackberry tarts their mother made – but they did deserve a treat, didn't they?

# Star Reads
## Series 3

Magical and mischievous tales from Fairyland and beyond...

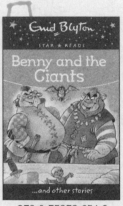

978-0-75372-654-9

978-0-75372-655-6

978-0-75372-656-3

978-0-75372-657-0

978-0-75372-658-7

978-0-75372-659-4